SOCIALLY SATISFIED

By
Beth Gelman
©Beth Gelman 2023

Copyright © 2023 by Beth Gelman
All rights reserved.

No part of this book may be reproduced or transmitted in any form or by any means, electronic or mechanical, including photocopying, recording, or by any information storage and retrieval system without the written permission of the author, except where permitted by law.

This is a work of fiction. Unless otherwise indicated, all the names, characters, businesses, places, events, and incidents in this book are either the product of the author's imagination or used in a fictitious manner. Any resemblance to actual persons, living or dead, or actual events is purely coincidental.

Interior Design by Frontpage LLC

Publisher: Cindy Ziegelman Enterprises LLCZ

ISBN: 9798378447299 (Paperback)

Summary: Ella & Viktor meet online at an off-brand social media site. Ella fantasizes about meeting Viktor, an up-and-coming actor in Los Angeles. She knows that she'll never actually speak with him though she hopes, just maybe, he might be the one on the other end of her private message. When the conversation turns intimate, Ella knows that she was speaking with him directly and not a computer bot. Viktor has so much to lose by taking a chance and trusting Ella with his heart and his career. He puts it all the line and shares his deepest thoughts with Ella hoping she will respect his privacy and his reputation. They grapple with the "what-ifs" of continuing their conversations and taking things to the next level.

[1. Romance 2. Contemporary romance 3. Romantic Fantasy 4. Social Media Love Affair 5. Love conquers all]

First Edition

Table of Contents

CHAPTER 1 5
CHAPTER 2 16
CHAPTER 3 21
CHAPTER 4 26
CHAPTER 5 33
CHAPTER 6 40
CHAPTER 7 57
CHAPTER 8 68
CHAPTER 9 77
CHAPTER 10 85
CHAPTER 11 92
CHAPTER 12 103
CHAPTER 13 112
CHAPTER 14 128
EPILOGUE 139
Acknowledgments 150
About the Author: 152
What's Next? 154
Sneak Peek: The Perfect Voice 155

BETH GELMAN

CHAPTER 1

ELLA

I lost another patient today. Not the whole patient, just part of them. This was the third one this week and it was only Tuesday. Why must people choose to play with fireworks? Haven't they realized it's all fun and games until you lose a limb? My most favorite lunacy I'd experienced was when this idiot used Independence Day to dare their idiot friends into doing more idiotic things like holding a lit firecracker and hoping he could finish chugging a whole beer before his hand blew up. Brilliant!

My shift ended at ten o'clock in the evening and as soon as I saw a man being wheeled down the hall on a gurney with his foot in a Ziplock bag. That was my cue to get the hell out of there. I loved my job. Most afternoons I dealt with rational people who truly needed medical help, a hand to hold while going through a difficult time in their life or a voice of reason to get them off their diabetic ledge of despair. I knew my job well and what lane to stay in to keep out of trouble. I shut my mouth when I didn't need to be involved and spoke my mind when I felt my opinion mattered the most. These were the joys of being an emergency room nurse.

"Hey, Ella. Mind staying and helping with the dingbat who decided he needed to chop down a tree at the same time he drank a case of beer?" Dr. Neilson pleaded.

This was not the first nor the last time the head doctor of the ER would beg for my help. I turned him down again. I had already picked up half a shift for a friend of mine earlier today and I wasn't staying a moment longer.

I pasted on a big smile and piled on the sarcasm, "You know how much I'd like to Dr. Neilson, but my pumpkin is waiting outside and if I miss it, well, you know what happens." I pursed my lips together, swished my chestnut ponytail in his direction, and did a one-eighty toward the locker room.

"You don't know what you're missing." He called after me and gave me what he presumed was an irresistible grin. Blech. This guy had more baggage than a train conductor.

He had been trying to get me to go out with him for two years. He would have had better luck snagging a newbie nurse to fawn at his feet. He was a hard no for me. No dating in the workplace. That was my policy.

Back in the locker room, I stripped out of my nasty scrubs and washed my face. God knows what splashed onto it throughout the day. I saved my showers for home, that way I could luxuriate and decompress on those especially difficult nights. Tonight, I was picking up Chinese and watching a Rom-Com on Netflix. I should probably be out hanging around with friends or family, except by the time I got home, showered, and was presentable again, it was almost midnight. Lately, though, I felt lonely no matter who I was around.

With my body exfoliated and my jammies on, I poured a glass of wine in a secondhand bubble-style wine glass, grabbed my Chinese take-out, and crossed the room to my favorite spot on the couch to slurp my Ho Fun noodles with some chopsticks. I nested myself into the cushions and picked up the remote and pulled the app. The best part about not having a boyfriend was not having to fight over what movie to watch and who had control of the clicker. I enjoyed being single these past couple of years even if I didn't have regular sex. Scheduling conflicts were no joke in my world. My hours made it difficult for most guys to manage, so why even try?

The realization of my chosen field also meant that I wasn't going to get rich quickly. I rented this apartment at a reasonable rate after I started working at University Hospital as an ER nurse. I had a queen-sized blowup mattress in the middle of the living room, pleased that it doubled as a bed and a couch. A card table acted as my dining table and the windows were adorned by a beautiful set of flowered percale sheets. It screamed, "Hey, I just graduated from college and am fifty-thousand dollars in debt." I was alone and never home, so who cared? It took me six months to buy a regular set of dishes, glasses, and flatware instead of Salvation Army specials, wine glasses excluded.

Six months after that, I traded my blow-up mattress for a bed and my parents lovingly took pity on me and bought me a new couch from one of those mega discount shopping places. That gift took the place of every birthday and Christmas gift for two years. I was grateful though. I was five years out of school and making decent money now. I had the emotional support of my parents to help me when I felt down, which happened to be happening increasingly more often. I considered getting a cat except I was afraid it would steal my breath when I slept. Probably an old wives' tale. I also considered a goldfish, though it wasn't much of an emotional support animal.

Last year I met a girl at a co-worker's party, and she needed a cheap place to live. Shira was a flight attendant and traveled two hundred and fifty days a year and only needed a place to store her things and a place to flop every few days. Since I lived twenty minutes from the airport, I offered her my living room and a pull-out couch and much to my chagrin, she accepted my offer. While I appreciated the occasional companionship, I appreciated the additional seven hundred dollars a month more. If I can convince her to stick around for three more years my loan will be paid in full.

    I digress. I've been dying to watch "The Spy in The Night" for three weeks now. Viktor Zolof was the lead actor and he was smokin' hot. His performance in his last movie was not only filled with swagger and stunts, but it was also heartfelt. If he was half as sensitive in real life as he was onscreen, I would swoon. I was banking on this film being more of the same and hoped that his career was gaining traction given there were so many more platforms that were producing films. I watched a couple of YouTube video interviews to learn more about him and I was pleasantly surprised that the accent I thought I'd heard was in fact from his Ukrainian youth. Don't ask me why that made him hotter, but it did. While the opening credits began, I trawled through my social media in hopes of finding any juicy bits about what he was up to this week.

    My phone interrupted me to check one of my social media accounts and I set my carton down precariously on the arm of the sofa, paused the movie, and slipped off the couch to pour another glass of red before I checked to see the notification that came through. Back in my couch-nest I crisscrossed my legs and cradled my phone in both hands. Truth be told, I'm more of a voyeur than a commenter. I liked to see how excited people, mostly women, would get after a hot picture was posted. Some of the crap they said ranged from crude to lewd and well past disgusting. These sites needed editors.

I'd been watching a few actors and actresses myself on all the popular social sites but I loved the Talk2Me site the best. Viktor was showcased often without a shirt, on-set, or modeling underwear. I could have stared at his form all day. Broad bulging shoulders and biceps, and pecs that screamed to be rubbed. To have a chance to massage my hands all over his body would be a dream come true.

His only flaw was that he had gorgeous women on his arms all the time. I wasn't jealous exactly because I thought they might be in a relationship with him, it was that I would never have a chance in hell myself at meeting a guy like him. The women that got those guys are all rail thin, botox'd, and boob lifted. I suppose I could also add that they had proximity, and I did not.

For most of my adult life, I thought being five foot six was a perfect height. Pair that with my C-cups and chestnut brown hair and toned body from all the competitive swimming I did when I was in high school, I passed as good-looking. My previous boyfriends made a big deal of my looks though I knew many girls much prettier than myself who fared far better in the dating pool. I thought I looked better than average. "Strong German genes," my dad would say. Whatever.

Lately, I thought of stepping out of my shell to try and communicate with my actor "friends." I'd often wondered, okay fantasized, about one of them answering my message themselves and not a bot, or their PR person. What would it hurt to click on their private message icon and send them a mildly interesting note? I set my expectations low and hoped maybe I would get a real response. I threw caution to the wind and sent Viktor a message. I'd Googled his image several times when I felt horny, especially after two glasses of wine. My long sex draught left me needy and susceptible to fantastic bouts of naughty dreams that weren't going to get fulfilled on their own. It was time to take action.

I grabbed my phone, said a prayer, and typed, "Hey, Viktor. If you're actually on this feed I'd love to chat." I pressed the send button thinking how lame that sounded. Suave was not my forte. I'm a lousy small talker, although if past experience held true, a few drinks never hurt my game, so perhaps tonight I might get lucky. Ten minutes went by and my movie was starting to pick up and I ogled Viktor's everything. He may be hot, but I wasn't going to wait all night for a reply so having heard nothing ten minutes later, I gave up waiting, paused my movie, and carried my junk back to the kitchen to clean up.

I moved my little party to my bedroom and finished watching the movie after I brushed my teeth and crawled under the matelassé duvet. My mind wandered waiting for a response from my lame text until I could feel that warm ethereal place between awareness and sleep wash over me. My phone pinged again and I sat up like a lightning bolt. *Where was I?* I reached over to grab my phone off the nightstand to see you who was bothering me so late.

"Hello, beautiful lady." Oh my god, he actually responded. I shook my head and screwed my fists into my sleepy eyes. This had to be one of those messaging bots trying to make me think he was really speaking to me. Fine. I'll bite. My inner teenage girl was thrilled with the hope that maybe it was Viktor responding so it didn't matter that my ability to reason this time of night was questionable.

"Hello. Did you have a good day?" *Ugh!* I sounded like his mother.

Time went by without a reply and I was fed up waiting. *Stupid bots.* I fell back to my pillow and waited one more minute with my arm hovering over my head staring at the screen. Nothing. I dumped my phone somewhere in the sheets giving myself a pep talk that sleep was more important than this experiment. I flipped over and within moments fell into a deep slumber.

Gifted with a bladder the size of a pea, I woke up and stumbled down the hall into the bathroom. Recently I installed a night light after I walked into the door frame after a particularly hard day at work. My coworkers thought I had been beaten up, and even my Charge Nurse, Rose, visited me later that night to be sure my life wasn't spinning out of control.

"Ella, is there anything you'd like to talk about? Anyone mistreating you?" Her eyes pleaded for an honest response.

"No, Rose," I bellowed. "It's this fucking job that's killing me. No more double shifts, I can't function for days afterwards." I whined at her and flapped my hands all around my head like a lunatic.

When I got back to my bed, my phone was lit up and my belly fluttered. I knew I should ignore it but hope springs eternal that the real Viktor would reply.

"Actually, today was a bitch."

Holy Shit! That was a real human reply, not a bot. Could this really be Viktor? Seriously, why would he write back? Maybe it was his PR person, or some other poser preying on hopelessly devoted fans?

I typed a response, and then deleted it and tried again. I sucked at this online flirting thing. Truthfully, I sucked at all flirtatious activity. I needed a cute reply without being too intense, yet interesting, but didn't vomit everything in my head.

I bit my lip and tried again.

"From your postings, it sounds like you have a lot on your plate. Want to talk about it?"

I looked at my clock. It was two thirty in the morning and a long conversation would take its toll on me at work later, yet I wanted, needed, to see if I was really talking to Viktor.

My phone pinged again and my heart rate soared.

"Where are you calling from?" *Shit!* It was bot.

They wanted to stalk me and find out my identity, empty my bank account and make the next five years of my life a living hell. I shouldn't have started down this path. What was I thinking? I know I'm acting stupid to respond this way, but something deep inside me said it was the right thing to do.

Feeling snarky, I replied, "Does it matter?"

His immediate reply shocked me. "Yes, it does. I'm on the west coast of the United States and if you're in Malaysia it's the middle of the night. I don't want to bother you."

He doesn't want to bother *me*? This was no bot. The compassion I saw in his eyes when I studied his pictures was truly him. He chatted with me!

"That is very thoughtful of you to ask. I'm in the States but in a different time zone. It's okay, though."

He responded immediately. "That's good to know. I have no idea who you are or if you'll believe anything I say. Your profile picture is quite beautiful. I hope you know I'm sincere when I say that."

He thought I was beautiful. *Damn!* I felt like a sucker falling for his words. He didn't know me at all. It's like saying you're only going to have one slice of pizza, and before you know it, you've eaten half of the pie.

Can he see me blushing? "Thank you. You're pretty sexy yourself." Sending that message had my heart soaring and my thighs squeezing together. Seriously, what could come of this? I'm going to enjoy it if nothing else.

I propped myself up on my pillows pulling my knees up to hold my phone and waited for his next reply.

"That's nice of you to say."

"I watched a few interviews of you on YouTube. You have a slight accent. Did I hear correctly that you're originally from Eastern Europe?" I wanted him to know that I knew a few things about him.

"Almost, Ukraine. Things were heating up politically when I was young and my parents decided it was time to get out before it became too difficult."

My face scrunched up hearing that. "I'm so sorry your family had to go through such difficult times. I am happy that you've made a good life for yourself here in the States. Are your parents well?"

My compassion as a nurse got the better of me. I knew that patients needed love and support to heal, and that had to be true for a struggling family who didn't know our language well or at all.

"How kind of you to ask. Yes, they are both still with me. We are very close."

Should I ask him why his day was a bitch? Should I ask more questions about his family? Better yet, I should sign off and get some sleep like a responsible adult. Nah. I was in this for the long haul, and quite frankly, this was the most action I'd had in six months.

"You mentioned you had a difficult day. Can I help at all?" I'm sure there was nothing I could do except listen. That's helpful, right?

"Yeah. Well…it turns out show business isn't as glamorous as it sounded. I won't bore you with all the ins and outs just know that everyone wants a piece of you and at the end of the day, you don't have much left for yourself."

Whoa. That was heavy. This had to be him. Even a poser didn't have time for this kind of reality show. He sounded tired and disgusted. I knew that feeling.

"Viktor, I can empathize. I'm an ER nurse, and I too, am pulled every which way. How are you handling the pressure? Do you have an S/O or sibling who can help you?" There had to be someone he could trust.

"I don't have time for relationships, and I don't have any siblings. Talking to you is about as much of a relationship as I can fit into my life right now. I'm sorry if that's too much to hear."

"It's not too much to hear. I'm sorry you don't have someone you can confide in. I'm happy to listen so you can vent if you think that would help?" Seriously? I'm just some overworked nurse in a crappy apartment. There had to be someone else in his life whom he could lean on.

"At the cost of sounding pathetic, I don't have any friends that I could trust not to exploit me for a payday. Believe it or not, I've always been kind of a loner."

Never in my life would I have taken him for a loaner. Girls had to have hung all over him his whole life, though that wouldn't mean he found their company fulfilling in some way.

"LOL. You? Pathetic? Hardly. That would be me. Nice try selling me on that." I'm still not sure I'm speaking with Viktor directly, but whoever was on the other side of these texts sounded very interesting.

"Really? Why are you so pathetic then?" Times up! He pushed my panic button. I wasn't sure I wanted to divulge that much information during our first chat. That kind of information seemed like a second or third conversation.

I yawned and stretched like a cat before sending my last message.

"It's been great messaging you, Viktor, but I have to get some sleep. I hope you find a confidant that values you as a person and not a payday."

I waited for a few minutes reviewing our conversation thread then finally got a reply.

"I already did—you. Sleep well, beautiful lady."

CHAPTER 2

VIKTOR

The banging on my front door was hostile and regular. My assistant woke me every morning because I didn't hear my alarm clock. Nicki was hired for me by my agent to make my life easier, except quite frankly, he was an asshole who made my life more aggravating.

"I'm coming. I'm coming." I wish I trusted this guy to give him a key but I don't. I don't trust anyone, not even my agent. I've been burned before with bullshit promises of people being responsible and dedicated, and let's not forget discrete. I was tired of being taken advantage of so the only person who got a key was Marianna, an old, respected friend of my parents who was my housekeeper, cook, and eagle eyes.

I slipped on a pair of athletic shorts that settled on my hips and skipped the t-shirt. I scrubbed my crop of hair and yawned until I squealed as I shuffled from my bedroom to the door.

"Good morning, Mr. Zolof. Did you sleep well?" As if he cared. I should make a recording and save him the trouble of opening his annoying mouth.

"Morning, Nicki." I didn't bother answering his question. He didn't care and I wasn't wasting my spit.

I turned and walked to the kitchen to start the coffeemaker. Marianna wouldn't arrive for another twenty minutes to make me breakfast, and I needed to take a shower.

"Leave my task sheet on the table, Nicki. Do me a favor and look up what an ER nurse does and print it out for me. I'll be back shortly."

I stepped into the shower dreaming of a woman I met online. Her profile picture showed long reddish-brown hair swept up at the sides and long dark lashes on an oval face. She was beautiful and from her photo, her shoulders seemed trim and her neck a creamy white. It was her lips that made my shower take longer than usual. I grabbed my aching cock and pulled several times thinking of her pink bowed lips that spread invitingly across her face. That smile would take my whole cock in and that thought had me coming hard and fast. I pressed my hand to the frosted glass wall to steady myself as I milked myself dry. Miss Ella would be on a loop in my mind for the next foreseeable future.

She was compassionate in a way I hadn't experienced in a long while and it gripped my chest to think perhaps this woman was more than a beautiful face. She let me into her life through the empathy she shared. I shouldn't have said as much as I did, but for some unexplainable reason, I felt a connection between us. I'm sure it was wishful thinking, though the subtext of our text said more than just words. I would find out if she felt the same way.

I slipped into the kitchen and poured myself a cup of coffee. Marianna was making my usual high-protein breakfast and I took my seat at the table.

"What did you find out about ER nurses?" I directed towards Nicki.

He slapped a piece of paper on the table and sat down with me while I read it.

"What's all the interest in ER nurses? Are you going to be playing one in a role soon?"

Efficiency wasn't the only thing Nicki was good at, being nosey was the second. He would leak this information to a friend of his who worked at a gossip rag and then every ER nurse in the area would stalk me.

"Not at this time. I watched a show last night and I was intrigued." Hopefully, that would throw him off and leave me alone.

"Hmm. Listen. You have a full day today. You have an interview with Good Morning L.A. at ten that we're late for. Two fittings for your next roles. A PR event at three, and then some retake filming from five to nine this evening. Craft services will feed you at seven o'clock. I'll have a protein smoothie for you though to power you through to the end of the night. Anything else?"

"Yeah. Send flowers to my parents. It's their anniversary today. Make it big. Three hundred dollars and throw in some chocolates." I grunted out my orders and wished I had time to find my own assistant. I was tired of his attitude and having to watch every word that came out of my mouth. This was my home and my sanctuary from all the Hollywood yahoos.

"Sure, boss. Meet me in the car in ten minutes. I'll call the studio and let them know we are on the way."

Every day, the same thing. Barely a breath between obligations and a bunch of white noise that meant nothing. The only thing on this day that meant anything besides acting was speaking with El30MG on the Talk2Me app later tonight. I needed to know more about her. She needed to believe I truly was who I said I was.

In the past, I tried to reach out to my fans on social media, but then things got ugly. Threats that I was sleeping with someone's wife to sculptures that wanted to make mini models of me to sell as idols. WTF? I turned all that over to my PR specialist and kept off social sites for several months. I found Talk2Me late at night a few weeks ago and posted two old pictures of myself at the beginning of my career. Most of my fans stayed on my official sites, but a few had branched off to this one. El30MG must be one of them. There wasn't a lot of traffic between midnight and six in the morning. Even so, most of our conversation last night was in a private message.

I blew through half my day only giving attention to the person in front of me. The other half of the day I conjured up scenarios I would act out with my late-night fan, should we ever meet. By the time the director yelled, "Cut. That's a wrap." I was flying off the sound stage grabbing my phone and my script for tomorrow's shoot. More often than not there were a few people who patted my back with praise, my director being one of them.

Gregory Randolf, a very prolific director, was a dream to work with. He gave you his vision, you delivered it, and you were done. If you had input, he'd listen. If the line wasn't working, he had it rewritten. The only time I saw his ire was when my co-star, Lannie Simone, showed up forty-five minutes late to set, keeping us all waiting. Let's just say she never did that again.

"Viktor, do you have a minute?" For this guy, yes. I smiled and turned toward the legend of a man.

"Of course, Greg. What's up?" I knew when to placate and when to keep walking.

He put a hand on my shoulder and stared into my eyes. Now I was nervous.

"Listen. I have a project I'm working on that I'd like you to read. I know you have Ukrainian lineage and wondered if you'd like to play a spy. I know it sounds cliche but there is a good twist you'd appreciate." Greg's eyes glazed over I assumed he was envisioning his new creation.

"Go on." I crossed my arms and took a wide stance while I started to piece how this story might unfold.

He pulled me over to his director's chair and had me take a seat. I loved this guy but I wanted to get out of here five minutes ago. I hoped this was worth my time.

"Imagine a spy gets sent to America to track down an essential component for a chemical weapon. The spy infiltrates a large pharmaceutical company and ends up falling for a hot blonde pharmaceutical representative. She ultimately thwarts his plans not only stopping his mission, but distracting him with her cunning, beauty, and quick wit derailing him from his scheme."

I pressed my lips together contemplating his offer.

"Sounds interesting. Yeah, send over the script to my agent and I'll take a look at it. Thanks for thinking of me." He patted my shoulder again and I took that as my cue to leave.

If Gregory wanted me in his next film, you could bet that the script will be at my agent by the morning. A working actor was a happy actor. I texted my driver and went to my dressing room to wash my face and change out of my costume. I'd be home by ten and God-willing, El30MG would be back online too. I had a million questions including the one she evaded last night.

CHAPTER 3

VIKTOR

The *Solyanka* Marianna left in the refrigerator was a lifesaver. She'd make a batch of this traditional stew that reminded me of my youth. My mom taught her several dishes to make and freeze for me so I would have something familiar when I felt alone. I heated a bowl and carried it into my living room to eat off my coffee table. I liked sitting on a cushion on the floor. It quite literally grounded me at the end of the day. I went back into the kitchen and poured three fingers of vodka into a crystal highball. As an afterthought, I also opened the fridge for mineral water. It was hard to stay hydrated knowing you couldn't leave the set to pee.

It was almost midnight, and I got more depressed as the night wore on. I really thought she would log on and we could continue getting to know each other but there was no sign of her being online. I cleaned up the living room and kitchen and walked down the hallway when my phone pinged with a notification.

She was back. Yes! I sounded like a pimply teenager waiting for the cute girl in class to talk to me. She even went straight to the direct message room which was very encouraging. I needed to calm down and get my head on straight.

"Hi, Viktor. How was your day? Better I hope." She remembered I had a shit day yesterday. So sweet.

"Hello. Today was much better but long. Thank you for asking." Be polite and not pushy, Viktor. "It occurred to me you know my name though I only know your call sign. Would you share yours with me?"

There was a long pause. I was a shithead! I scared her off.

I was pressed for time and needed to get into the shower and then get ready for bed. If she was going to stall we would lose our window to chat. Of course, as soon as was soapy and wet, I heard my phone go off. Time for the world's fastest shower.

A one-word response, "Ella." Beautiful Ella.

"Thank you for sharing that with me. That's a beautiful name. Tell me about your day. What does an ER nurse do?" I was desperate to know more about her. The blurb Nicki found was perfunctory and I wanted to understand what being an ER nurse meant to her.

Another few minutes went by, then she replied, "It was a pretty good day. One of the staff had a birthday which meant we all had cake for lunch. A family whose son had an appendix out came to say thank you for identifying the problem so quickly and getting their son to surgery without delay. Appreciation like that goes a long way in our business" She signed with a smiling emoji with three hearts around it. Delightful.

"That's terrific. I'm happy you are surrounded by good people around you." It sure beats what I deal with every day.

I wanted a picture to look at, not the tiny profile picture that barely showed her face.

"How would you feel about sending me a picture of yourself? I can hardly see your face in your profile picture and I'd really like to look at it while I speak with you. I'll send you one too if you want. Just, please don't share it with anyone." If I wanted her trust, I'd have to offer something of value to prove I trusted her.

"Um, are you sure you're not a stalker? This is kind of freaking me out still."

The only way I could convince her was to send her a selfie of me. She had to know it was not someone sliding in a picture of me to fool her. I tousled up my hair and propped myself up in bed. No shirt with the sheets covering my lower half. I gave her a sexy smile and snapped two pics. One with my arm behind my head with a bulging triceps straight on and the other off to the side.

"Wow! It really is you. Um, you look amazing." She said with a blushing smiley face to boot.

"I wanted you to know it really is me you're speaking with. My agent would have a cow if he knew I was having this conversation. They like to monitor everything I do. It's very annoying." I laughed to myself knowing how disobedient I was being.

"Well, thank you for your trust. I'll guard it carefully. Here is a photo of me."

A minute or two went by and there she was. Decked out in a light blue tank top and if I zoomed in could see the outline of her areolas through her tank top. Fuck, that's hot. Her gorgeous hair hung in waves over her shoulders and her blue eyes danced for the camera. She had a small nose and a natural smile that lit up her face. And, like her profile picture, I could see more clearly her bowed full pink lips. I loved those lips.

"Damn, girl. You are stunning. Thank you from the bottom of my heart for this. I don't get the chance to meet many people outside of show business. It's great to see what a non-self-absorbed woman looks like."

"How do you know I'm not self-absorbed?" She taunted me. Fine. Let's play.

"You would have been telling me all about you and what you want, and you wanted it, and what you wanted from me by now." Truth.

"You're right about that. I don't want anything from you, Viktor just some companionship if you want it." This girl was a dream come true.

I had a million questions for her that would scare her off, so I went out on a limb and asked this one question before she signed off and I'd never hear from her again.

"Ella, you ended our conversation last night when I asked you why you thought you were pathetic. You don't sound pathetic. You sound compassionate and kind, and I'm sure if I heard your voice, it would be sexy. Why would you feel that way?"

More time ticketed by and my clock informed me it was past twelve-thirty. We both needed to sleep except I wanted an answer tonight. This woman was anything but pathetic. She had a story and she needed to share it with me. This wasn't a one-way conversation.

"Viktor, to answer that I need to divulge a lot more information, and I'm not sure I want to do that at this time." She was on the defensive again.

"Ella, please, I'm a safe person. Whatever you think you are, you aren't. Please trust me. Give me anything." I begged for any grain of information that I could hang onto until tomorrow night.

I turned off my nightstand light and adjusted my pillows to sleep when my phone pinged again.

"I'm sure I'll regret this, but here goes. I'm a thirty-year-old college graduate living in a studio apartment in the Midwest, living paycheck to paycheck, and the only friends I have are from work and a guy online."

At that moment, I realized she and I were living the same life. I went to college for public health and ended up understudying for my roommate in a play he was in. He had mononucleosis and couldn't finish the play and at his request, he contacted the director begging for me to be the stand-in since I ran lines with him all the time. Ta-da! My acting experience in a nutshell.

"I think we are living parallel lives except my relationship is with a female, not a male." I included a sideways laughing face to lighten the mood.

"LOL. We are a sad pair."

Another long-shot question. "What do you think about committing to an online relationship, Ella? You and me and the ether?"

No response.

"Sleep on it. It's time to get some rest beautiful. Thank you again for your honesty. It's refreshing." I rolled back to my nightstand to plug in my phone and put it on vibrate. It didn't make a sound again that night.

CHAPTER 4

ELLA

I laid in bed rehashing our brief conversation. It amazed me how much we could cover in such a short amount of time. Viktor got right to the point. I couldn't believe that I sent him a selfie with an almost threadbare tank top. I wanted to lick my phone looking at his bare chest it was so yummy. His six-pack rippled across his lightly tanned skin and his happy trail peeked just above the line of covers draping his hips. Damn, he was beautiful.

Describing my behavior to anyone would make me look like a teenage girl with ridiculous hopes of meeting her heartthrob in the flesh. I knew that wasn't going to happen, it's just that the thrill was intoxicating and addictive. It was like the lottery, we played knowing we wouldn't win the big jackpot except we kept feeding the pot until it got big enough, we thought the financial sacrifice would pay off. Someone had to win. Why not me?

I stayed up staring at my phone for another thirty minutes. Lost between reality and fantasy weighing the pros and cons of my actions. My heart continued to say, "Follow me! Have fun, take a chance," though my head kept reminding me of the opposite, "Don't be a loser thinking anything will come of this. The person texting you could still be a stalker ready to pounce making my life a misery."

In the end, I fell asleep looking at his sad beautiful eyes and delicious mouth. I woke up early with my hand inside my panties. I was wet and wanting and I needed a release. I reached inside my dresser for my trusty vibrator. Old Faithful never let me down and I wasn't too proud to admit how necessary he was to my mental health. I needed relief from my throbbing clit and the dual action buttons were the only thing that gets me off as quickly as possible. My heart pounded in my chest as I came calling Viktor's name. I pinched my nipples hard thinking of him mounting me and fucking me deeply, his balls smacking my ass each and every time. Please God, if ever I get a chance to fuck this man, do NOT disappoint me with his performance. How awful would it be to build him up looking like he does only to have him be a colossal disappointment in bed? *Horrifying!*

It was Saturday and I had the day off so I enjoyed rolling in and out of consciousness until after ten. Nothing says fun like spending your day off doing my weekly cleaning chores and laundry. Every load brought up new questions to ask, as well as how many of his questions was I prepared to answer. What did he mean by 'us being committed?' How would that even work out? I'm over two-thousand miles away and in a different time zone–two time zones. We've only messaged each other for less than an hour twice and the thought of us being a couple was ludicrous. If he was a real live person in my life we would most likely not have this discussion for, I don't know, weeks, right? I should just ask him what he was thinking. Maybe I'm thinking something totally different? Maybe I was delirious thinking online line texting was real life? My dad was right, I really am immature.

Two hours later my inner child won, and I typed out a message.

"Hey. I know it's not our regular time to chat except that I finally found the courage to answer your question…with a question."

I waited a few minutes to see if he would respond. He had to be busy with something work-related. Or maybe he was visiting with his parents. Either way, he wasn't…

PING.

"Good morning beautiful, Ella." I loved it when he said it like that. I'm projecting his response in a thick Ukrainian accent–slow and sexy.

'Good afternoon, Viktor. Are you busy?" He was a star, and I was a simple midwestern woman. Of course, he had more important things to do than waste his time talking with me.

"I'm never too busy for you." Man, I would have liked to have seen his face in person while he said that.

"Thank you. That is very sweet of you to say. I do have a question for you, though. What exactly did you mean my 'us being a couple?' How would that even work?"

No response. Five minutes later, still no response. *Argh!* I flipped the laundry and started folding my clothes doing my best to not get emotionally strung out from the lack of a text message.

PING.

"I'm so sorry for the delay. My assistant just came by to drop off my dry cleaning and I needed to get rid of him. To your question, first, we could talk on the phone, then face-to-face online, then if you wanted, we could, escalate things. Online first, then… maybe…we can find other opportunities to communicate."

Gulp. Escalate? Like-sexting? Or dating each other online? Was he suggesting that we have video sex? In fantasyland that sounded so fucking hot, but in real life would I actually do those things? I'm no porn star and I certainly didn't want anything I ever said to go viral, especially with my clothes off. I was leery, to say the least, but turned on–hell yeah.

"You intrigue me, Viktor. Whether we were in person or not I'd want to progress our relationship slowly. I don't have any desire to be in the limelight while we are getting to know one another. Would you be okay with that?" I hoped he would be. I was having too much fun with this man even if I couldn't tell anyone.

"I'm very okay with that. Will you agree then that you will only have a relationship with me? I don't share very well" *Holy shit!* The good thing about me being me, was that I could barely hold down one intimate relationship let alone two, so Viktor just won the jackpot on my fidelity.

"I agree," I said, fighting back the urge to laugh.

"I'm messaging you my phone number. Please send me yours and I'll call you right back. I'm desperate to hear your voice."

"Me too," I admitted and sent him my number.

OMG! I'm going to be talking with my heartthrob in a matter of minutes. I wish I knew how to prepare for this. Crap! I had to fix my hair and put on some make-up. I was halfway to the bathroom when I realized we would be speaking on the phone and not on a video call. Whew! All my carefully crafted messages were caput. He was going to get full-on Ella. I hope I don't screw this up.

His number popped up on my phone screen and I paused to relish this moment. Ugh! I'm such a loser. I accepted the call and I'll never forget the first words he spoke to me.

29

"Hello beautiful, will you be my girlfriend?" My panties gushed and I felt faint. I sat down at the kitchen table running a hand through my hair trying to get my bearings straight.

"Hello, Viktor. I can't believe I'm really speaking to you." My voice cracked and I rushed to get some water. He sounded exactly like his interviews and on the big screen. I'm sure I'll sound like an idiot any minute now.

I chugged several ounces of water and tried to put a coherent sentence together.

"I would like to be your girlfriend. Too bad we can't hold hands and walk along the beach to commemorate the moment." Dream on, girl.

"One day, Ella. I will walk you down a beach. Count on it." He purred.

Christ! Everything coming out of his mouth makes my thighs clench.

I hummed into the phone. "Careful what you wish for. I could end up being a pain in your ass before that happens." I tried to lighten the mood except I sounded self-deprecating in the process.

"Let me decide what I think of you, okay? So far you sound radiant through the phone." I could feel his sincerity and I blushed to let his words blanket me in joy.

"What are you up to today?" Our conversation needed to be more than compliments to each other. I wanted to know what a movie star did on the weekends.

He laughed. "Well, today is unusual in that I don't have any appearances to make, and since I don't have to be on set until Monday, I'm doing my laundry and then will go to the gym."

"On my god, you're doing the same thing I'm doing. We're so domestic? I'm meeting my parents for a bike ride through The Dells in an hour and we'll spend the rest of the day touring around and having dinner." I put my phone on speaker and began to fold towels to distract myself.

"Have you had Ukrainian food before?" He added a very heavy accent to the word Ukrainian, rolling the "r" and making me swoon.

"Uh, no. Besides Vodka and cheese knish, I haven't had any Eastern European foods, unless you count German food. I eat lots of that. What foods do you like?" I countered.

"I love most foods, including spaetzle. I knew we'd get along well together." He laughed again. "What's a Dell?" He inquired.

Many people have heard of the Wisconsin Dells though I'm sure all they think about are cheese curds. It's not that they were wrong, it's that they had no idea what a dell was.

"A dell is a glacier-cut impression that melted away the earth into small hollows and valleys covered in grass or turf. I know I sound like a dictionary, except people still can't visualize them unless I explain it that way." I blathered on too long. He'd never ask a question of me again.

"That's fantastic!" He shouted. "The only dells in Ukraine that I know about is a computer company." His laugh was throaty and deep and very enticing.

I loved his quick wit. He was funny and I liked the sound of his voice as it reverberated in my chest.

I responded, "You're very funny, Viktor." I smiled brightly even though he couldn't see me.

We chatted about each of the cities we lived in, a few work tidbits, and the members of our family general until I had to leave.

"I wish I could stay and talk longer but I need to get out the door. This has been wonderful. Truly." I effused as much appreciation into my voice as possible.

"Dear Ella. You have filled my heart today. Hearing your voice makes what we started so much more real. Thank you for spending time with me." He sounded a little choked up.

I wish I didn't have to go. I'd rather have stayed to ask about why this was so emotional for him. "Enjoy the rest of your day…boyfriend. I'll be thinking of you at the gym." Yeah, girl. Let him know he'll be on your mind.

Then he hummed. "Dosvidaniya, Ella." And he was gone.

CHAPTER 5

VIKTOR

She's amazing. I still can't believe she took a chance on me and gave me her number. I could talk to her all day. I wanted to talk to my parents just in case something went sideways and she ratted me out to the paparazzi. I wanted nothing more than to trust her implicitly except I've been burned and it hurts too much to do it again, except...

I bought my parents a home down in Lakewood and made the drive with my sunroof down and my radio blaring. When I entered the gated community, I saw dozens of people riding bikes, chatting and strolling along the sidewalks. This place had all the amenities like golf, pools, a clubhouse, and a bar. They worked incredibly hard to get us to where we are today and taking care of them now meant the world to me. Now they could relax, make more friends, and enjoy the fruits of their labor.

"Pryv'it Mama, pryv'it Poppa." I kissed both their cheeks and gave them a big hug.

As much as I am Americanized, my parents still keep to their old country ways. It makes them feel good when I accommodate them that way. Mama always made three meals when I came to visit and all the leftovers came home with me complete with directions for Marianna on how to warm them up. I had quite a compilation of Ukrainian dishes and authentic Italian food lining my freezer as we speak. Now, if only I had a cook, I could be self-sufficient. Another downside of being an actor.

"Viktor! It's been too long." Their English was good if not occasionally broken in places.

"It's great to see you both. Listen. I have something to run by you and wanted your opinion." My mother gestured to us to the patio out back and retrieved the coffee service from the kitchen. Ukrainians did not talk about anything unless coffee was present, that was unless vodka was required.

My father was first to speak.

"So, tell me *kokhanyy*, what is on your mind." My father took a biscuit off the plate mama brought from the kitchen. He still looked at me like I'm his darling little boy.

"I've met someone." Of course, their eyes blew wide open. They were only thinking of the grandchildren I've been negligent in providing to them. I'm almost thirty and they had been bugging me about meeting a good girl and giving them some babies to love for five years now. *Give me a break.*

"Listen, don't get ahead of yourselves. I just met her three days ago and we don't live in the same city let alone the same state." I put my hand up to slow them down. When they sat back in their seats I continued.

"Her name is Ella, and she lives in Wisconsin. That's two time zones away. She is an emergency room nurse and is very beautiful. She's a real down-to-earth person, Mama. I think you'd like her." She slapped her hands together in front of her heart glowing at the news.

I pulled at my day-old stubble and braced myself for the punchline to this story.

"The real issue with her is that—we met—online." I locked eyes with my father wanting to dissect every emotion that passed through them. He was the gatekeeper of this family and even though I was a grown-ass man, his opinions mattered and could shut this whole fantasy down.

"Online, like one of those dating sites? You are better than that. Why would you stoop so low, Viktor?" *Here we go.*

"Poppa, that is how a lot of people are meeting these days. I don't have the luxury of meeting regular people. If I took a date to a restaurant, any place for that matter, our evening would be full of me signing autographs, flashbulbs in our faces, and interruptions. It's impossible." I pleaded my case including that I can't be on dating sites or social media like everyone else.

"Darling, how did you find Ella then?" She queried softly.

"It was just a freaky cosmic thing. I was on a small almost unknown social site at midnight and so was she. She didn't believe me when I said it was me speaking to her, not a computer bot or a public relations person. She was still a little skeptical until we spoke to each other on the phone. She's really doing a number on me, Mama. I might even want to meet her one day."

I flopped back in my seat grabbing another cookie as I hit the cushion. It did sound far-fetched, and they would be right to think I was out of my mind, but when the words came out of my mouth, they sounded comfortable and right.

My father sipped at his coffee staring into its blackness like a crystal ball. (Yeah, I could use some answers too.) Moments later he set his cup down and leaned forward over his knees steepling his fingers in the space between his knees.

"This all sounds very unorthodox. When we were growing up, we never had this as an option. Someone knew someone and poof you were married. If you think that she is an honest respectful girl and your gut tells you she's good then you should have more conversations with her. Who knows what will come of this? Try to understand who she is and how she thinks to know whether she will be a good match for you. We trust you, son. Thank you for sharing this with us."

My father stood up and came around the coffee table and pulled me up for a big hug. My mother got up as well and kissed both of my cheeks.

"Will we ever have a chance to speak with her too?" My dear mother pleaded like this was my last hope with a woman.

"We'll see, mama. Let me meet her first, okay?" I laughed and gave them both another hug.

Two hours later and six containers of food, I was back on the road to my apartment. I kept hearing Ella's voice in my head, and it was driving me crazy. I looked at her picture when I got home, and I had to speak with her. I couldn't wait until late tonight. I scrolled to her name that I entered into my phone a few days ago and went out onto my balcony to enjoy the ocean view. It rang three times and went to voicemail. *Damn.* I left what I thought was a sweet message though I suppose she could construe something else from it as well.

"Hello, my Ella. I'm sorry I missed speaking with you. I was–um–just wanting to talk with you again and hoped you'd be available. You're probably working. I need to talk with you face to face. I need to see your mouth when you speak to me. I need you to —show me how you feel about me. I don't have work today. Call when you can. I'll be in the gym getting sweaty. Bye."

I sounded so desperate. What am I sixteen? I hope she...what? What did you hope she would say or do, asshole? I stormed my way through the apartment to my bedroom and stripped. I grabbed a pair of gym shorts and a tank and went to the basement gym with my shoes untied. I needed to pump all this frustration and lust out of my system. I had to purge the anxiety out of every pore and hoped she was who she said she was. How could I fall for someone I met online only three days ago? Shit, we only had one conversation where I could hear her voice. More importantly, why did I think I would find a woman, woo her, and convince her to date me exclusively after two conversations? I'm ridiculous!

I entered the gym with my apartment fob and did a forward fold to tie my shoes and stretch out my hamstrings. A few more stretches and I jumped onto the treadmill for a ten-mile run then some weights. I pushed myself far beyond my regular workout chastising myself and trying to be realistic about Ella and what our relationship could be. By the time I was finished, I was drenched and light-headed. I chugged five cups of water from the water cooler and went back up to my apartment for a protein shake, a cold shower, and waited like a child.

My phone pinged as the blender stopped and I grabbed it fast as I could thinking it would be Ella, except it was Gregory

Randolf. What did he want? Wiping my mouth with the back of my hand, I answered his video call.

"Hey, Gregory. To what do I owe the honor today?" I sounded so snobby.

"What are you doing next weekend?" He demanded.

"Uh, not sure. I'd have to check with my assistant. What were you thinking?" My interest was piqued.

"Remember that project I told you I was working on? Well, we have the studio's blessing and I want to take the primary cast to see the location and do some preliminary takes. You know scene and lighting tests. Only three days and then I'm not sure at this point when the official shoot will begin. Depends on the prelim outcomes."

I was shocked. I hadn't even gone in for the reading he asked me to do yet. I don't even know if he spoke to my agent. This seemed very unusual even for this wackadoodle.

"Wow, Greg. That's fantastic." Never tell the director he is wackadoodle. You have to finesse them, at least that's what my agent has taught me.

"Have you even spoken to my agent? I thought I was coming over this week to read for you. Am I cast already? Don't I need a contract?"

"Listen, son. I've been in this business too long to have to wait for all that crap to happen. The studio said 'go,' and I'm going before they change their mind. I'll call your agent as soon as you give me your schedule for next weekend. Are you in or not?" His furry eyebrows hiked up his forehead like a caterpillar and his lips pursed. He pointed his index finger directly at me as he spoke for emphasis.

"Uh, well, yes. If we can get a contract together by Thursday, sure. Hey, where in Wisconsin are we going?" I leaned against the back of my couch hoping, no praying, it was near Ella.

"Fitchburg, Wisconsin. Twenty-five minutes from the airport. Why, do you need to know?" I heard a car door shut and him yelling at someone to watch what they were doing in the background.

"Just asking." I punched the air spilling my smoothie down the side of the glass.

"Whatever. Get back to me ASAP." He growled into the phone. This guy was a chameleon. When he was on set, he was cool, calm, and collected, but outside the studio, he was a crusty old bear.

"You got it. Thanks again for the opportunity, Gregory" I hung up and texted Nicki and my agent to contact me ASAP.

I wasted no time texting Ella. I had to speak with her immediately. I had to let her know my plans. This time next week I would have her in my arms and kiss those sexy pink lips. If it were up to me, I'd have her in my bed every moment I wasn't on set planting myself fully between her creamy thighs. I guy could wish, right?

Nicki responded five minutes later and my agent called five minutes after that. I was going to Wisconsin. I just hoped Ella wouldn't freak out when she heard the news.

CHAPTER 6

ELLA

"You'd better hope Dr. Neilson doesn't see you in that dress. You know he has a thing for you, right?" Rose pulled her glasses off and gave me a once-over. Twirling her finger around in a circle she demanded I give her a three-hundred-and-sixty-degree view.

It was my parents' fortieth wedding anniversary that required me to swap shifts so I was able to leave the hospital by five o'clock. My flirty sundress in cobalt blue was the complete opposite of what most people saw me in, especially this crew. My breasts were high, and my strapless bra was barely concealed below the plunging neckline and halter top. My sister insisted that I get this dress knowing we would be at a fine dining restaurant and the whole family would be there including a friend of the family that had made it clear he was waiting for me to "take him as a lover." Every time I remember him saying that, because it wasn't a one-time thing, I vomited a little in my mouth. I hadn't seen most of my family since I graduated from high school so I'm pretty sure they'll be shocked to see me as an adult.

I did a slow spin for Rose under her assessing gaze.

"Can you recognize me? I'm a woman in women's clothing. It's like a disguise that no one would see through." I pressed my lips together chuckling.

Her finger stopped twirling and both hands struck a pose on her ample hips.

"Uh, yeah. You had me fooled. I don't know if I'd recognize you on the street. You're looking fine." Her seal of approval washed over me and I blushed. I don't get compliments often especially coming from a fifty-year-old married woman.

"Thanks, Rose. That means a lot to me. Have a good night and I'll see you Wednesday." I grabbed my duffle bag with my work clothes and walked out to my car.

Settling into the driver's seat I took my phone out to check that my family didn't need anything and happily saw a text from Viktor. Oh my god. He's never contacted me during a workday. Duh? You just gave him your number crazy lady.

I stopped abruptly outside the revolving hospital door and nearly collided with a little old man in a wheelchair. He's what!? Coming to Wisconsin? Next weekend? *Shit.* My fantasy life just turned into a reality show. What was I supposed to do now? I can't take off work. What will I wear? Will he want to...? Yeah, I really want that too. *Time for a full-body waxing.*

He sent me this message a while ago so he's probably waiting for a response. And say what? "You absolutely should come and fuck my brains out." *Now I'm just being silly, but really*...I made five attempts at a text and I finally crafted a message that didn't make me sound like a lunatic or a ditz.

"Viktor. Wow, what a great surprise. I'd love to see you when you come in. I'm not sure I can change my work schedule though. I'll do the best I can." I applied a coat of lip gloss, fluffed my hair, and checked my mascara in the rearview mirror. Make-up and I had an understanding. If it took more than five minutes to apply, I wouldn't use it. That left me with a natural look all the time. Mascara, lip gloss, and eyeshadow. That's it.

I pulled into the parking lot of La Brasserie and parked next to a lamppost. My dad insisted from the beginning of my driving days that if a space was available under a light, park there for safety. He was right. I'd heard too many stories of girls being attacked in unlit parking lots to do it myself. My phone rang rattling me from my paranoia and Viktor's ID came up on video chat. Thank God I was put together. I didn't want to scare the poor man.

I answered trying to get the best angle for my face. I ended up propping it up on my dashboard. He could see me behind the wheel and all the way down to the seat. Showtime.

"Viktor, hi, what a surprise. Two in one day." I said happily.

His face slackened from his smile and air escaped his mouth, but nothing came out.

"Are you all right?" He looked floored.

He gulped and licked his lips. Those gorgeous plump lips.

"You look incredible. He rubbed his jaw, his eyes boring into me.

I blushed and licked my lips, too. I cast my eyes down as he appraised me. By the smoldering look on his face, he liked what he saw.

"Thank you. I'm going into my parent's anniversary dinner in a few minutes so you caught me at a good time." I babbled some more details until I sounded stupid. "Sorry. It's just that we have never spoken to each other live and it's kind of freaking me out." I twisted my hands together in my lap hoping he wouldn't see them.

"You're right. It is our first time talking live and let me tell you how impressed I am with you already."

What was I supposed to say to that? I bit my lip demurely and hoped he'd continue.

"So…you saw my text. It would be incredible to meet you next weekend. Would you be okay with that? I mean, we won't have much time together since we'll be doing some preliminary shooting. You could visit the set or I could pick you up from work and we could hang out. Whatever you're comfortable with." He rushed his speech out getting redder by the sentence. He was adorable. This big hulking man who blushed as if he was asking a girl out for the first time. Well, first time for me, I suppose.

"I'll make myself available as much as my schedule will allow. This is a fantasy coming true. I never thought I'd meet you in person. Are you sure you want to hang out with a boring girl from the Midwest?" By the look on his face, my deprecating comments didn't go over well. His eyes radiated pain. I blew it! It was bound to happen. I hate dating.

"Ella, I never want to hear you say things like that about yourself again. You insult me by thinking I am too good, or that

I don't know whom I want to spend my time with. I chose you without ever having seen your face. You have captivated me through your humor, intellect, and sexy voice. You needn't apologize to me, ever."

Wow! I felt so stupid. I slumped back into my seat to contemplate what he just said. Self-deprecating thoughts weren't sexy or appealing, even when I heard someone else doing the same thing. When I heard the words leave my mouth, I knew I sounded weak and pathetic. I never felt that way about anything else in my life, why am I letting these thoughts in my head now?

I dug deep and found a grain of self-respect and gave him my eyes again.

"You're right. I'm sorry. From what I've seen and read you have impeccable taste, it's just, I can't get my brain to bridge the gap of a movie star wanting to spend time with me. Please forgive me."

He smirked. "Honestly, I just don't want to spend time with you."

My eyebrows raised in uncertainty. "So not just having dinner or going for a walk?" I was pushing my luck asking that question. I needed to know what to expect next week and he just alluded to something a lot more intimate.

His smile grew to reach his brown eyes. Fuck was that sexy.

He ran his hands through his dirty blonde hair and looked into the camera just like in a movie. "If you'd let me, I want to touch you…everywhere."

OH. I almost passed out as a bolt of electricity connected to every limb of my body. I wiggled in my seat to find my panties soaking wet. He just can't say stuff like that to me and not make me all tingly. His eyes hooded over, and I felt mine flutter at the thought of his hands sliding down my body cupping my breasts and kissing me like I was his last meal.

"Viktor." I purred. "You're killing me over here." I rubbed my lips together and ran my hands down my thighs.

"Sweet girl. You have a party to go to, and I have to speak with my agent. Be a good girl and have fun. I want to see you one more time in that dress before you take it off tonight." The husky hum of his words and his dark eyes scrambled my brain. My whole body clenched at the thought of him seeing me taking off my dress. *Mmm.* Would I do that for him? I barely knew the guy. It was the look on his face, his hooded eyes, and the pulse of my desire that commanded my body to say, "yes, yes, yes."

"You are an evil man leaving me like this. Go and speak to your agent and I'll call you later tonight." I managed a cogent departure and hung up.

I sat in my car until I could see straight and not like I'd had a joint as an appetizer because God knows I wanted to fuck that man. Hard.

Dinner was fantastic and the way my parents still looked at each other, filled with love and appreciation, was something I would strive for with a man of my own one day. I just needed to get past the first date. Finding Viktor online was more in line with finding Easter Eggs at a Theme Park, difficult, yet once you did, each one was a treasure. I tried a couple of times to feel out the waters of online dating with my sister and Aunt Rose except both agreed it was disastrous and dangerous. Of course, my sister is already married to her high school sweetheart and my aunt is pushing ninety. That's how I felt until I met Viktor. Was I making a big mistake? Probably. I may have bitten off more of my fingernails at dinner than the linguini. If Ralph, our family friend looked at me one more time mouthing disgusting things, I was going to use my forks like Ninja stars and throw them at his obnoxious face.

Shortly after the cake cutting, I hugged everyone goodbye and walked out with my older sister, Missy, arm in arm. Missy and I had always been close, and her opinions always helped me to make good decisions. I needed a confidante and I hoped again she would be up for the challenge.

We stopped in front of my old Honda, and I pulled her in tightly for a hug. It was time to tell her my tale.

"Hey, Big Sis, I need your help with something." I pulled back and looked into her light blue eyes. "I may be in a relationship." I bit my lip embarrassed.

Her eyebrows shot up, "Maybe in a relationship? Are you, or aren't you?" She went immediately into interrogation mode. "Did he ask you, or did you ask him to be your boyfriend?"

I rubbed my forehead. "He did ask, and I said yes, but that's not the problem." I expelled the rest of my air.

Exasperation dripped off her tongue, "El, come on, I have kids to get home to. What's going on?"

Fine. "I met someone online and we texted for a while and now are speaking on the phone, and we just had our first video chat earlier today, now he is coming to town for work and wants to meet me in person." This sounded like an episode of Find Me a Foreign Bride.

Missy winked her eye at me and put her hands on her hips in what looked like a proud sister moment. "Way to go 'Lil Sis. What's his name? Where is he from? Give me all the details." She shook her head and egged me on.

"Well–he's from L.A…and he is gorgeous…and was originally from Ukraine." Would that be enough for her to figure this out? God, I'd hope so.

"And…his name?" She begged.

Apparently, I needed to spell this out for her. I shifted to my other foot and looked down at her polished toes.

"Viktor Zolof," I whispered, fidgeting with my fingers. I slowly looked back to her blank expression, his name not ringing a bell.

I needed to leave and clicked my fob to open my car. Missy followed and gave me a big hug. "Good luck, El. Try and have some fun for a change." She winked at me again and crossed in front of my car. So much for finishing this conversation.

I had put the car in gear when I heard a giant smack to the hood of my car. Rattled by the sound, I put the car back in Park thinking I hit an animal or a child, but it was Missy. She ran back around to the driver's side, Viktor's name finally registered on her face. I rolled the window down to screams of disbelief.

"*The* Viktor Zolof? The hottest guy in show business? The actor that pulls you in with his eyes and takes you hostage

Viktor?" She was manic pacing along the driver's side of the car and I had to hold back a chuckle.

I grabbed my phone and opened my picture gallery to show her the one of him splayed out on his pillows. She clutched the side of the car and swooned into the window.

"Bitch! I hate you. How the hell did this happen? How am I supposed to go home to my regular hot husband when you have Adonis coming to visit you? We are so double dating. I'm not taking no for an answer." I was laughing so hard I think I peed a little in my panties. She could have, should have, been an actress. Her comedic timing was spot on.

"I can't guarantee that since he will be working most of the weekend. How does a signed headshot sound?" I goaded her just for the fun of it.

"How about you forward me this picture, so I have something to enjoy when Dennis is traveling?" She waggled her eyebrows in a very naughty way.

I shook my head. "That's a hard no. If I have a chance in hell at making this relationship work, I have to honor his request for privacy. It's really hard being a public figure, it's the reason we found each other."

She cupped my chin and gave me a kiss on each cheek. "You always were the trustworthy, reliable sister. I think it's terrific you found each other. I'm rooting for you both." She waved goodbye and rolled up the window thinking about how lucky I was to have a sister who would take my secrets to the grave for me.

By the time I made it home, I was exhausted. A full day of work, a party, and a lot of sexual tension wiped me out. I walked into my bathroom, flipped my hair back onto my shoulder, and leaned forward to brush my teeth. Thoughts about the impending video call I was about to make had me jittery and so distracted I almost brushed my teeth with cortisone cream.

He wanted me to wear this dress for our call, and I wanted to take it off for him. That's probably the wine from dinner talking, though the image of me doing something that reckless was titillating. My sister was right. I was a good girl who always followed the rules and colored inside the lines. Viktor brought out a hidden woman lying in the shadows wondering if she was strong enough to break free of her known persona. This was my home, and I could do what I wanted in it. I guess I'm the petulant child desperate to have her way this time. Well, damn it, I would have my way. With all the courage my self-talk could muster, I dialed Viktor's number and prepared myself to be a siren.

The phone rang and rang, and with each trill of the ringer, my resolve lessened and lessened. I dropped the phone on my lap just as I heard his voice.

"Hey. I wasn't sure you would be able to make tonight's call." I pushed my brown tresses behind my ear and propped the phone on my nightstand phone holder.

His eyes pulled at me through the screen as if luring me more into his spell. Missy was right.

"Sorry for the delay in picking up. My director had some notes for me that I couldn't blow him off. How was the party? Congratulations to your parents."

I told him about the evening as I walked with my phone to my closet mirror and turned the perspective around so I could show him my complete silhouette. I can honestly say that

I hadn't had a man in this bedroom since I moved in a few years back. The couch maybe, the kitchen table definitely, but never anything this intimate in my bedroom.

"Damn, Ella. You're gorgeous." His Ukrainian accent thickened with every word he spoke. "Turn around. *Mmm*. Stunning." He dragged out every word, each one more thickly accented than the last.

"Thank you. I suppose I do it justice." I replied, not wanting self-deprecating comments to come out of my mouth again.

"Ella," he dragged his hand over his jaw, his eyes studying my face for what?

"Ella, I want to push you a little. Would you let me do that?" His once-brown eyes burned with an amber glow. He pulled off his t-shirt and my heart stopped. Fuck he's hot.

I nodded in reply since my vocal cords couldn't make a sound.

"I want to see you out of that dress. Would you do that for me?" How do you say no to a god like him?

I took my phone holder and walked him across the room to my dresser and arranged the view so he could see all of me. I was in a dream watching a girl perform for a master puppeteer. He was in complete control of the situation, and I let him. It was so freeing not to have to think about right and wrong, good, or bad. I took comfort in that I could shut this down anytime I wanted.

"Viktor. I don't know if I'd do this for anyone but you." I whispered and untied the bow behind my neck letting the halter fall down to my hips. I heard his breath thickening in large hefts of his pecs.

"Fuck, Ella. I wish I could pull your hips to my own. I'd suck your tongue and kiss you until we both passed out. I need to touch you; I need to touch myself." He was positioned again on his white fluffy pillows and he licked his lips as he watched me push my dress down to the floor.

His shoulders bulged as he slid his pants down his body and he pointed his camera at the very large bulge of his boxer briefs. He grabbed his cock and squeezed it through the fabric, moaning my name as his eyes hooded over.

"Look what you've done to me, baby. I've been fantasizing about you all day." He kept staring at me in amazement and squeezing his rather impressive cock.

Feeling more confident, I decided to put on a little show for him. He was the actor, but I could get into a role too for the right person, and Viktor was definitely worthy of this performance.

I came closer to the phone and licked my lips for him. I reached behind me unclasping my bra and slowly peeling each cup off my aching breasts then letting it fall to the floor. He moaned again and slid his hand inside his underwear. I could see the tip of his cock just above the elastic and I moaned back.

My eyes glazed over and were lost in the moment. "Christ, Viktor, I wish I was there to lick that pearl off your cock."

He took that moment to yank his underwear down and his dick sprang free.

My jaw dropped and my hands smacked over my mouth.

"Shit, Viktor. Do you have a license for that thing?" I chuckled pinching my nipples into tall peaks.

"What the fuck are you talking about? Do you have a license for those things? They're huge. Fucking fantastic." He dragged each word out matching his strokes to the length of his cock.

I blushed at his description. My tits were pretty impressive. In ninth grade, I went from an A cup to a C cup in one summer. My chest hurt so badly that my mom got me a salve to rub on them to reduce the pain and the only thing that salve did was to turn me on twice daily.

Another moan hummed through the phone followed by another command.

"Baby, please show me your pussy. Show me how pretty it is." I loved his pleas. The more we pleasured ourselves the heavier his accent became, and it was sexy as fuck. I ached to have his hands on me.

"Since you asked so nicely, I'll give you a complete tour of my pussy." I winked and spun around for him to see my ass. My white lace thong barely covered my crack, and given the hissing sounds from Viktor, he was liking what he saw.

"Is this okay, baby?" I bent down so that the camera was only inches away and if he looked carefully enough could see the beauty mark I had next to the crack on my left ass cheek.

"You're perfect. So. Fucking. Perfect." His deep purple erection pulsed and jerked and I knew he was close to coming. I was fascinated with how his body contracted and released as he pulled at his erection. He licked his lips and clenched his jaw stopping me from my task. I couldn't take my eyes off him.

"You're magnificent, Viktor," I whispered, and my heartbeat double-timed.

I hooked my thumbs into the sides of my panties as I slid them down slowly pressing my flat palms down my thighs giving him a Marilyn Monroe curtsy.

"You're bare!" He bellowed. "God damn it. I knew you would be. Fuck me, Ella."

"I wish I could!" I yelled back. I was out of control. Things were coming out of my mouth that I would never have said and my hands danced over my skin making me feel like a goddess. I wanted to see him come. I wanted to see him lose control, and I wanted to be the one to do it to him.

I pushed closer to the camera and with both hands gently pulled my pussy lips apart so he could see my clit. See how red and swollen I was for him. I wanted him right this moment, but I would have to wait another week to know what he felt like on my skin and mouth and…

"Rub it for me, baby. Rub your clit slow and lightly and think of my tongue flicking it." I did what he said and I groaned my approval. "That's right, baby. Think of me doing unspeakable things to make you come." He gasped as he commanded me to obey.

"Viktor." His name was a prayer on my tongue. "Please, I want you to fuck me. I want you inside me." I begged repeatedly. I looked at what I was doing into the camera and saw how erotic and filthy I was but stopping wasn't an option. I needed this. I needed him.

"I knew you were a dirty girl, baby. I knew we would be great together." He grabbed his balls with his other hand and massaged them eliciting a painful hiss from his full mouth.

"I'm going to come. I want to come with you." My mouth was parched, and I was a wreck pulling my orgasm from my throbbing pussy.

"Yes! Ella, yes! Come, baby. Let me feel your walls clench down on my cock." He grunted out his final command and I exploded into a million tiny pieces. I had an out-of-body experience I couldn't explain and he watched me as I melted back into the sheets. So erotic. I'd never orgasmed like this; so hard, so fast, and completely fulfilling. I watched him shoot his load all over his stomach following the cords of fluid that reached his pecs. I felt proud to have done that to him. Fuck! I really am a dirty girl.

"Baby girl. That was spectacular and smoking hot. I want you so badly again. Did you like it?" He was so complimentary, making the moments afterward so appreciated. It didn't feel like a horny couple getting off, it felt refreshing. No attitude or rushing to get his pants on to leave like the assholes I dated. He felt so comfortable in his skin that he made me feel comfortable in mine.

I played with the sheet and decided to wrap it around me still albeit a little embarrassed about how wanton I'd become. He couldn't know how exposed I felt. Shit, I'd never been pushed like that or allowed myself to be in the moment letting myself go. Of the few guys I managed to have sex with, they were only interested in what turned them on, let alone what I needed. I needed to do this again, preferably in person.

I held my phone and touched his face on the screen. I licked my lips as if I'd reach through the plastic to his mouth and traced it with my own tongue.

"What we did was beyond anything I had ever done in the past. You have this way of pulling me out of my mind and making my body feel like putty in your hands, except you haven't even touched me yet. Are you sure you're a mortal man and not some wizard overlord?" I laughed quietly.

He laughed in response. "A wizard, huh? Ella, next week I'm going to put you under a spell that you won't want to get out of. You're blowing my mind and I don't want to overwhelm you. Just know that it's not your body that attracted me initially. Your heart reached out and held mine when I needed it the most and I'm afraid that if you decide you want out of this relationship that it might stop beating." He placed his hand over his heart, and I expelled every ounce of air in my lungs. He needed me. Not just as a plaything, he wanted more. Is that what he was saying?

"Viktor, I–I am deeply touched by your words. I don't want to be anywhere else or be with anyone else. You seem to understand me in a way no one else has. I can't wait to see you." I blew him a kiss and placed my hand over my heart mirroring his sentiment.

"I've never met anyone like you, baby. I can't wait to see you in person, too. Sleep well, beautiful Ella. I'll be dreaming of you."

Damn this guy. He always knew what to say to get me to swoon. He was perfect, and when he turned on his Ukrainian-controlling side, my insides clenched and my panties became soaked. I'm a lost cause.

"Goodnight, Viktor," I whispered touching the screen again.

We stared at each other without speaking. We turned off the lights and climbed under our covers and stared at each other some more. I don't remember ending the call, but I did hear something about falling. What was falling?

CHAPTER 7

VIKTOR

I stared at her face remembering how she looked when she came undone; chest heaving and her hands raking through her silky brown hair. I'd been with my share of women, all who have had their charms, but this woman was so pure in her release and expression of pleasure that it captivated me. Her long lashes fluttered dreamily, and the way her mouth fell open begged to suck my cock. I wanted her on so many levels and in so many ways that I was pissed that I couldn't get my fucking hands on her. I think I'm falling for her.

I kept the line open not having the strength to end our evening and fell into a thoroughly deep sleep. I hadn't had one of those in months. What felt like moments later, I heard a gasp and bolted upright. I heard a voice and looked around my room for the source when I heard my name coming up from the sheets.

"Viktor." My phone whispered. "Over here, it's Ella." She waved her fingers at me.

I shook my head trying to get my bearings and looked over by my pillow and saw the source of my confusion.

"El? Wow, I-I must have forgotten to hang up the call last night. I was, uh, watching you sleep and must have dozed off." My face burned with embarrassment and I laughed.

The corners of her lips bowed upwards and her eyes gleamed behind smudged makeup. She pushed her swarm of hair behind her ears and mumbled something.

"I sure hope you weren't staying up all night to see my bedhead. It's a good thing we're on a chat or you'd be running away from my morning breath." She quipped adorably.

I fluffed my pillows and leaned back to soak in her loveliness. Even disheveled, she was more beautiful that any woman I'd ever seen.

"You're stunning. It would be my deepest pleasure to wake up to your morning breath, provided you'd stick around for mine. Or maybe we should make a pact to keep mouthwash on the nightstand so we don't have to get out of bed? What do you say?" I gave her one of my leading men's smiles and hoped she'd succumb to my fabulousness.

"Hmmm. Sounds enticing. Perhaps we should invest in a spittoon for when we're finished?" Very cheeky. She leaned forward over her pretzeled legs exposing her perfect breasts under a loose tank top.

"Sweetheart, I'll invest in anything that would keep you in my bed. This will be the longest week of my life. Would it be okay with you if I stayed with you while I'm in town? I don't want to miss a moment with you." My puppy-dog eyes were made to get people to do what I wanted. She had to say yes or I would bang on her door all weekend.

"Well…are you housebroken? Those puppy dog eyes are very convincing." She bit her lip with a smug laugh huffing through.

I threw my head back with a loud booming laugh. She was hilarious and I loved how playful she was. If she only knew how I wanted to play with her.

"Yes, baby. And, more than that, I'll roll over for you anytime you want to rub my belly–or anything else for that matter." My smile stretched from ear to ear, pained from the joy she brought me.

"Fine. I'll take you in, but you have to take me out to dinner first. I'm not one of those Hollywood groupies that does anything for nothing." She stripped off the sheet uncovering her lower half and showing me her full-cheeked ass as she left my field of view.

"Hey, get that fine ass back here! I'm not done looking yet."

"Hang on! I have to pee!" She bellowed from across the room. I heard the water running and less than a minute later she picked up the phone again. "Patience, please. You can't have all of me all the time. I have obligations and responsibilities, and a small bladder," she giggled.

"I'll see everything when I stay with you in five days and eight hours." I couldn't control the angst in my voice. "I wish I could blow off all my appointments and shoots this week. Promise me you'll clear out your weekend for me." That sounded like begging.

"Send me your schedule and I'll do my best to work around it. Maybe I could watch you run a few takes?" She was fishing, but I was biting.

"Absolutely. You can even sit in my chair." I waggled my brows.

"Sweet!" She clapped her hands making the screen swish back and forth across her room.

I pulled the sheets away from my body exposing a very large and painful erection.

"Unless you have time to watch me jerk off to your tits, I'll say d*osvidaniya* and save one of these for you for later." I pointed to my dick but didn't wait for her response as I started getting myself off. I wasn't shy about my needs and she'll learn I have a lot of them.

She stayed and watched silently obliging me by removing her top. Her heavily hooded eyes told me of her desire as she rubbed her nipples between her fingertips. My groan was enough to startle her and she waved goodbye. Fuck that was hot.

An hour later I was face-to-face with my director via Zoom. We worked out the details of our three-day trip now turned four. I wanted time with Ella and he could work anywhere he had Wi-Fi. I emailed her a detailed itinerary of when I'd be available and when she could sit in and watch a few scenes. Her response was hot, "As a special thank you for getting me onto your set, I'd like to get you off on your set." Her devilish demand made my mouth water. "Scope out something special." Damn! This woman knows me better than I thought she did.

Nicki was back in my apartment at nine in the morning listing off all my appointments like a machine gun, while Marianna was blending a protein shake. It was my favorite morning show. Both of them vying for my attention, and not-so-obviously delivering barbs with their sass. Just like my childhood, except no one was yelling at me to shut my mouth.

"Viktor, you need to make a decision on whether you're going to accept that role for the action film that starts shooting in October. Their casting director is blowing up my voicemail." He pressed his lips together in annoyance like he was personally being attacked.

I too sighed my annoyance, "Tell them I'll have an answer for them next week." I have a relationship I need to vet and a different film that I definitely want to do but won't know if the location will work out. Seriously, how the hell can I predict what was going to be going on in my life in six months, let alone a year from now?

"Fine. You have a Today Show interview early tomorrow so please get to bed at a decent hour. The bags under your eyes tell me you're not following the sleeping regime I gave you."

I slammed my finished shake glass onto the wooden table and stood up abruptly.

"Nicki, let me remind you that although I appreciate your suggestions for a clean lifestyle, it's still my life and I'll live it any way I damn well please. Understood?"

He gulped and looked contrite. As he should. "Sorry, Viktor. It's just that I want you to look and feel your best every day."

Hmmm. "I'm sure you do. Anything else I need to know to get my day going?" I carried my glass back to the counter to the smug-faced, Marianna.

Nicki scoured his tablet for anything that was missed. "Nope. Everything has been covered except that your mom called and said she needed to speak with you as soon as possible."

"What!" I was pissed. He should have told me this first thing, not waste twenty minutes of my and my family's precious time babbling about shit that didn't matter in the big picture. I walked right up to his face which sat five inches lower than mine.

"Don't you ever put my family's calls at the bottom of your list like an afterthought. Do you understand me?" My finger was in his face and I hoped he would make some sort of smirk so I could punch his lights out. Instead. He gulped again and begged for forgiveness. I had to keep reminding myself this kid was only seven years younger than me; young, stupid, and entitled. "Enough for today. Leave and think about how you'd like to keep this job. Just because your aunt's husband works for a director, doesn't mean you're qualified to do it. Learn your place and your audience. Go!"

Not waiting for him to leave, I grabbed my cell phone off the breakfast table, clicked on my mom's number, and stormed into my den slamming the door behind me.

She answered on the second ring.

"Mama. My assistant said you had an urgent matter to discuss." I paced in front of my desk not knowing the severity of her call.

"Dorohyy. We have a slight problem and hope you might be able to help us." She sounded subdued in a way that I had never heard before. I grew concerned.

"Anything for you, you know that. What's going on?"

My pacing turned to stomping and I was afraid Marianna might think something was wrong so I forced myself onto the loveseat in front of the window.

"The U.S. Immigration office contacted us. They need us, all of us, to bring our passports down to their office tomorrow morning at eleven. Since the change in President, every immigrant in the past thirty years is circumspect. I'm sorry if this will cause you any trouble."

"Are you shitting me? I'm sorry for the swearing, Mama, but we have legal papers. I watched the man stamp it approved in his tiny office twenty-five years ago. I remember because he smoked so much it was choking me." I slapped my hand to my forehead which had begun to bead with perspiration. I needed to calm down…I needed to call my lawyer.

Mama, let me call you back. I'm calling my lawyer and getting the best immigration attorney money can buy. We are not going back to Ukraine. Please tell Dad I have this covered and not to stress. His heart can't take another hit." I rushed her off the phone with my love and my promise to make this right.

Two minutes later I was on the phone with my lawyer making plans to meet this afternoon with his friend, the immigration specialist, along with my parents. I placed another call back to my parents to fill them in, and, then stormed out of my den just like I entered.

"Marianna. Please set the table for four this evening and make your special filet for my guests. Make this meal your finest, please. Oh, and one of your amazing desserts, too." I smiled and patted her back as she preened knowing that she could show off her exemplary culinary skills.

I hadn't even showered and I'd made more high-level decisions in two hours than in my whole professional life. People depended on me and I wouldn't let them down. I needed to vent to someone. Someone who understood me and had no attachment to my career, or the optics of this situation, or anything. Just someone to listen and tell me everything will work out fine.

Ella. She would care and say the right things. I wanted to believe I could trust her so badly. All the lust and sex meant nothing if she didn't connect with me when things were difficult. I hoped these circumstances wouldn't damage our new fragile relationship, but life doesn't wait for perfect opportunities to show your feelings or convictions. They are inherently there or not, and it was time to find out how committed she was to this fantasy-gone-real.

Her phone rang several times and while I waited, I sat on the side of my bed. I prayed like I never had that what I saw in her was true.

"Viktor, hey, how are you?" she huffed into the receiver.

"I'm so sorry to bother you at work, El. I have an urgent issue I'm dealing with and I need to vent. Would you have a few minutes to talk?" My voice hitched and I swallowed hard trying to keep my composure.

"Let me call you back in ten minutes. I have a patient I need to discharge and I'll call you right back. Okay?" She was still out of breath giving me her reply.

"Of course. I'll take a quick shower and be ready when you call."

"Viktor?"

"Yes, sweetheart."

"Everything will be all right. I'll call you back in a few minutes." The phone went dead yet my heart soared. I knew she would say the right thing even without knowing my situation. I sprang from the bed and took the fastest shower of my life, dressing, and was back on the overstuffed chair that I kept in my room for reading.

My mind was racing with all the possibilities this meeting could impose. We couldn't possibly be forced from the U.S. We worked respectable jobs. My father taught at UCLA for twenty-five years, it was the reason he was able to get a work visa so quickly. He taught international politics and Ukrainian. He was a prominent figure at the university and was liked by everyone who knew him. My mother was an interpreter for a commercial banking organization. She traveled periodically around the country when dignitaries came to town, though that was infrequent. I was an A student. Never in trouble. I was always a perfect citizen, we all were. I couldn't understand why this was happening to us. Politics in this country was getting scarier by the day but I couldn't let it affect my family. Not again.

My phone buzzed and I immediately answered. To her word, Ella called me back. I would reward her for her loyalty as soon as I could get my hands on her.

"Viktor, are you okay? You sounded so upset." She exhaled slowly; a softness enveloped her words.

"Beautiful Ella. You are my savior. Thank you for returning my call as promised." I pressed on for efficiency. "It's my family. We are being asked to review our immigration papers tomorrow and my parents are in disbelief...I'm in disbelief." My exasperation was evident in my tone. I relayed the whole story of our immigration and our journey here to America. By the time I was finished, I heard a slam on the end of her line. "What was that Ella?"

"Oh! That was me banging on my locker. I'm so pissed off about this. Why isn't our government spending time on people who are obviously problematic instead of hardworking people who have only brought positivity to our communities? Viktor—my heart is breaking for you. Do you think this immigration person will make things right for you and your parents? Can I help in any way?" Her voice broke and I could feel the tears flowing in her voice. My girl.

"Baby, please don't cry. All of this will work out in time. I hope it's just a formality. Your concern and support truly mean the world to me. You have no idea. No one else knows about this situation so I'll need your discretion again. It will come out in the tabloids soon enough but hopefully, long after this ordeal is finished."

She sniffled her response, "Of course. You mean so much to me. I would never hurt you. Your secret is safe with me."

I could hear her trying to regain her composure when mine began to fail.

"Baby, we will see each other soon and I'll show you how much you mean to me. Please keep me in your prayers and I'll let you know how tomorrow's meeting goes." I whispered.

"Okay. Be strong and call whenever you need to. I-I…" I didn't need to hear the words now. We need to be in the same room for that. It was the way she struggled to hold back her emotions that gave me hope she'd felt the same way.

"Viktor, I need to go back to work. Please try not to fret about this too much. It will all work out, or I'll have to move to Ukraine." She laughed her comment off, but would she? It didn't matter, I'm not going back there, and neither were my parents.

CHAPTER 8

ELLA

"I really need this weekend off, Rose. I've never asked for time off. I've stepped up countless times to cover shifts for everyone else on this floor. Is it too much to ask for a couple of days off?" I crossed my arms under my ample breasts, stuck out my lower lip, and hitched my hip to one side. I'm smarter than a fifth-grader but I still could muster up a fifth-grade temper tantrum when I need to.

Rose pulled her readers down her nose giving me some stink-eye.

"Geez, Ella. Spreading it kind of thick, aren't you? He must be one amazing guy to whine like you are." She pushed her glasses back up and continued to click around on her computer keyboard. I stepped around the counter to see what she was working on, and to my pleasure, she had the nurse staffing calendar open and jotting down some information.

"Here." She snapped her wrist upward with the note. "You can have Friday to Sunday if you can get those people to cover for you. You've covered for each of them twice this year so they owe you. Good luck. Let me know by the end of the day what you find out. Her wink and smile were enough for me to bolt down the hall hunting for Dottie and Alan to cover my shifts.

Three patients and two, "you owe Me's," and I was back at Rose's desk waving that same piece of paper.

"Done! I've noted the shifts both Dottie and Alan will cover for me, now I just need your blessing and I'll be free when Viktor comes to town." I did a little dance with my hands in the air and my hips bumping the counter.

"So, his name is Viktor, huh? You've never mentioned him before," she probed.

Oops. I probably shouldn't have mentioned his name. "Uh, yeah. It's new but very promising. I'm trying not to get my hopes up but this weekend will be very telling as to whether our relationship will move forward. And, by forward I mean…well, you know what I mean." I felt my cheeks get red and I'm sure I sounded like a tittering teenage girl. I'm such a dork.

"Well, you tell Mr. Wonderful that he better treat you right, or Mama Rose is going to beat his ass." The way she jutted her chin out had me nervous for him.

"I'll deliver the message. Thanks, Rose. You're the best. Now I'm off to catheter Her Majesty, Miriam Donovan, in room three. She claims to be a distant cousin of QE2." With an eye roll and a shoulder hug, I hustled down the hall to prepare my patient for a not-so-comfortable procedure. Catheters on women were so much easier. Men are big babies about a plastic tube being shoved up their urethra. *Try shoving a kid out of a vagina?*

Several hours later my shift was over and as soon as I buckled myself into my car, my phone lit up with Viktor's face. Yeah, my magical powers did that.

"How did your meeting go? Will this go away easily? I got this weekend off. I'm yours for the whole thing." Breathe girl. Give the man a chance to answer.

"Can we video chat?"

"Yeah, I'm in my car." The video icon popped up instantly and I was looking at the most tormented beautiful man I'd ever seen. "Oh, Viktor. You look terrible."

He chuckled. "Thanks for cheering me up, beautiful." His lips pulled slightly as if in pain. "I wish I could tell you my meeting went smoothly, but I can't. It appears the date was left off the immigration officer's signature line and they won't accept the date my parents filled in on their line. It's a technicality. So now we have to wait until the clerk's affidavit can be taken. The good news is that that guy is still alive although he won't remember our case. It's just so stupid. The attorney I hired is working hard to sway the court to let it go since we have all been model citizens and our papers are otherwise pristine. Fuck! I'm losing my shit over this, and the worst part of our meeting was that we were advised not to leave the state until this gets resolved. That could be tomorrow or months from now. Either way, I won't be able to meet with you this weekend in Wisconsin. It's killing me to tell you this."

My stomach dropped and my mouth hung low in anguish. We planned for this. We ached for each other. I didn't want to whine about the inconvenience but my face must have signaled to him my feelings.

"I know, baby. I feel the same way. It's so unfair, but I have a solution you might be happy with. Would you consider flying out to see me? I'll pay for everything; I just need to hold you and feel your positive energy."

His face softened and he licked his lips in anticipation of my answer. How could I say no? There weren't any obstacles keeping me from going, except where would I stay? What if he met me and decided that I wasn't who he thought I was? I pushed my hair behind my ear and thought of the logistics of this trip, and my eyes lit up. I switched screens and pulled up the Delta App to see what flights I could catch Thursday afternoon.

"Viktor, I could catch a red eye to L.A. Thursday night and be there by seven in the morning. We wouldn't need to miss any time together and I could do the same coming back. My Monday shift doesn't start until three in the afternoon so–what do you think?" My hand was over my mouth keeping my trembling lips from his view.

"You're brilliant and beautiful. I'll have my assistant book it now. I'll have a car pick you up from your apartment in time for your flight and another to bring you to my apartment. You don't mind staying here, do you? I mean, I am going to keep you naked all weekend so don't pack much, and don't plan on running away from me either. I can be pretty intense sometimes. I just need you to communicate with me. El–I need you so much right now. I'm so happy you're in my life."

He was rambling, but so was my heart. My fantasy of Viktor coming to Wisconsin to visit me was just that, surreal. I couldn't believe I was packing for a real to visit my fantasy and it felt like the adventure of a lifetime. To think, just a few weeks ago, I was sitting on my couch playing at the idea of direct messaging someone completely out of my league, and today, not only am I choosing lingerie from a sparse collection that's been stuffed into the back of a drawer, but in three days I'll be face to face with the most gorgeous man I'd ever set eyes on. Please God, make him like me.

Twenty minutes later I looked around my room trying to think of what I might need for my trip when I witnessed what could only be described at Pack-A-Gedden. To be clear, the results of tearing through one's closet and dresser's randomly selecting clothing for a trip with unclear activities were what I was up against. I hadn't a clue where we would be going, who we would be with, and whether I'd need to pack a slip. I went with basics and a few accessories and hoped that would suffice. My intuition knew though that part of this trip would be meeting his parents. I needed an outfit that said, "I'm a nice girl with good values and made their son proud." The rest of my attributes would have to be learned through conversation. Besides high school, I'd never been introduced to my boyfriend's parents. I wasn't around longer than a few months to make an issue of it. I hoped this trip would be a game-changer for me. I really liked Viktor and I knew his parents' approval of me would be important to him.

Three days quickly went by and I was off to the airport to board my flight to L.A. when Viktor rang my phone on a video chat. It was dark in the limo, and even darker on his side of the call.

"I can hardly see you." I squinted my eyes straining to see him better.

He chuckled. "I'm in a supply closet off-set. I only have a few minutes before I have to shoot this commercial but needed to hear your voice and see your face to wish you a safe flight. I can't wait to finally have you in my arms." His throaty whisper sent chills through my body.

"I can't wait either. What product are you promoting?"

He hummed into the receiver, "Underwear." Yummy! I could imagine his fine form in tight boxer briefs.

"You're killing me here. Boxer briefs, right?" My imagination needed clarification.

Another chuckle. "No baby, these are European designs. Modal briefs and thongs that most men would run from."

"Shit. Now you have me all hot and bothered. Can you steal some and give me a fashion show later?" I bit my lip feeling a little embarrassed at my enthusiasm.

"Consider it done. They actually do amazing things for my libido." I could see his perfect white teeth grinning at me.

"Ah, your libido is just fine on its own, Mr. Zolof." Now I was grinning.

VIKTOR

My girl was getting on a plane to see me. My girl! As a good-looking guy, you would think I had chicks all over me from a young age, but you'd be wrong. I wasn't lying to Ella when I said I was a loner, people scared me and I kept to myself whenever possible. Had I not been found acting, I'd be locked in an office pushing papers.

This whole fantasy adventure was screeching to a halt and my head was ready to explode. A real woman was traveling across the country because of what I said to her. How I begged her to pivot on a dime and she didn't ask any questions. Who does that? I could be a psycho luring her to my lair to do horrific things to her. *Don't be an idiot.* You'll do naughty things to her that she'll die from pleasure from instead.

Seriously. I'm not an idiot. I did a background check on her and she was as squeaky clean as they come. Both my assistant and my public relations manager insisted that I at least do the bare minimum to protect my life and my image. Of course, the real reason was that they didn't want to have to find new employment if I died or more importantly, my career died.

Marianna made us a feast to enjoy all weekend along with simonizing the apartment to perfection. Fresh chrysanthemums and Birds of Paradise made the place look and smell like paradise. She would arrive in the early morning, so I had the coffeemaker on a timer so I could bring her a travel mug of hot java to wake her up. Initially, I was going to have my driver make the trip to the airport and changed my mind. Instead, I got my white Jeep Wrangler Rubicon detailed and gassed it up while driving to the airport myself, besides, I couldn't wait another minute to get my hands on Ella.

On the drive down the 105W, my hands started to sweat and I began to panic. What if she didn't like me? Maybe she'll be too smart for me? I'm not stupid but she's a nurse and well-educated. I happen to have a high IQ though I didn't finish college since my acting career started taking off. Ella didn't give me the impression she was a snob about such things, but who knows if our instant chemistry was as good as our digital chemistry. I hated those awkward moments. They weirded me out. My phone rang and my lawyer verbally vomited a bunch of information before I even said hello.

"Whoa, whoa. Hang on. Slow that down and let's try this again, Anthony."

His deep sigh indicated he was also rolling his eyes at me. Fine. Whatever.

"Your appointment has been moved from this afternoon to eleven this morning. Call your parents and be sure you're at the immigration office no later than ten thirty. We need to run through all contingencies and everyone must be confident in their answers. There can be no room for scrutiny. Do you understand?" His patronizing tone reminded me of my uncle, Boris. No one knew more than he did regardless of their rightness.

"I heard you, and we'll be there. Do you really think this tiny hiccup will cause my whole family to be deported?"

"Hmm. I've seen worse, but your notoriety will be an asset to our case."

"Small favors, I suppose. See you soon."

I stared at the horizon, my brain was numb and my body was jittery. Today would be the biggest rollercoaster I'd ever ridden. First, the Ella, then the immigration low. The whole thing was almost completely out of my hands and that was not how I liked to roll.

Another call flashed Ella's sexy lips on my screen. I snapped a close-up photo of her mouth when she was fingering herself so I never would forget her expression. Now my dick was hard and my mouth was dry from nerves hearing her voice paired with that image. I needed to get a grip.

"Hello, Viktor! I made it. I can't wait to see you," she said, her voice was giddy with excitement.

"Hey, baby. I'm so excited too." I grinned like a fool in love. "Come down to the International Level after you get your bag and my driver will be there with a sign. I can't wait to see you."

CHAPTER 9

ELLA

I only had a rolling bag and another shoulder bag for everything else so I asked a passing flight attendant if she knew where I could find my driver. I couldn't believe I was in Los Angeles. I wonder how many stars, besides my favorite one, would I see–meet. I daydreamed of what I'd say when I met them and more importantly when I met Viktor. First impressions were so important that I spent ten minutes in the ladies' room after I exited the plane so I could redo my face and fluff my hair. As I said before, I'm not a prima donna, but I do have some, okay a little, self-respect and wanted to greet my future something-something putting my best foot forward. Lips glossed, hair teased at the ends of my long brown hair to give some fullness, and a clean deep-V white t-shirt and tight-washed jeans would do the trick. I even went so far as to switch my shoes from cross-trainers to tan booties that matched my cropped suede jacket. I hope he liked my look because that's what this girl called her first dates finest.

My head swiveled as I stepped off the escalator searching for the placard with my name on it. I imagined an elderly fellow with a black cap and a black jacket except what I got was the hottest hunk in show business wearing a white t-shirt stretched mercilessly across his broad chest and wearing washed-out jeans that hugged his large, muscled thighs. *Shit.* I was in over my head. In my wildest dreams, I never saw myself with a guy like him.

I literally slowed my roll, staring at Viktor trying to unscramble my brain for who I thought would pick me up, and who actually did. I stopped in front of him afraid to breathe let alone speak. His sandy-brown eyes that crinkled at the corners when he smiled mesmerized me and I stood speechless for another ten seconds. He looked at me, too. Saying nothing. Absorbing my stare. Sharing our energy back and forth until he dropped his sign, grabbed my face, and kissed me hard.

My head spun and my knees gave way. This must be what all those women meant when they described swooning. It was quite heady, indeed. I needed him on a molecular level, though not in the middle of an airport. He must have sensed this too since people started recognizing him and a dozen phones snapped our pictures. "Welcome to the limelight, El."

He softly kissed me one more time and turned to grab my bag while taking my hand and pulling me along to the set of sliding doors behind us. He threw my luggage into the rear compartment of his Jeep and when he finally jumped in, we stared at each other again then broke out into laughter. We were like two kids who had kept a secret from the world until now and we were ecstatic about having finally closed the gap in our relationship.

"I could devour you right now. You're so beautiful and I'm so grateful to have you here." He reached over and brushed his knuckles down the side of my cheek. I purred like a kitten as I turned my face into his hand soaking up his praise.

"I can't believe it either. How did I even get here?" I took his hand in both of mine and kissed his palm." I continued to stare at him while he struggled to keep his eyes on the road.

"It's unbelievable, isn't it? We could write a movie about this and both be stars." He laughed brightly showing his even white teeth. "All I want to do is bring you back to my apartment and bolt the door shut for three days. I'm sorry all our time won't be alone. Do you forgive me?" His eyes became sad and his bottom lip bumped out looking like a sad puppy. My heart broke for what he had to go through and I prayed as I'd never prayed before that his immigration situation would go away.

He looked down at the console between us and handed me a travel mug. "Coffee with cream and sugar. I hope you'll like it. I can't start the day without it." He waggled his brows encouragingly.

I sipped the still-hot coffee and hummed my approval. "Thank you so much for this. It's perfect. When do you have to go to your appointment?"

"It got moved up from this afternoon to late this morning at eleven o'clock, except, I have to be there by ten-thirty to meet with my attorney. Since it's only seven-thirty now, how about we stop for breakfast and take a walk around downtown L.A. I'll show you some of the over-the-top shops and you can drool over all the pretty people." He took my hand again and kissed the top. "Or...we can find a secluded area and jump each other's bones for three hours." His big laugh triggered one out of me, too.

"You'd like that wouldn't you?" I winked at him.

"You know I would." He winked back.

"I'll tell you what, get me that breakfast you promised, and as so long as you leave some room in that flat belly of yours you can have me for dessert." Holy shit! When did I become a seductress? One fucking day out of Wisconsin and I'd become a wanton woman.

"Christ, El. You're on!" He stepped on the gas and we arrived at our destination ten minutes later.

True to his word, Viktor left chaff marks along both of my breasts, my neck, my thighs, and I'm ashamed to admit, my pussy. We drove down the highway and found a pull-off that seemed secluded enough for us to catch up. He threw the truck into the park, and hopped out before the dust on the road had cleared.

"Get out, Ella." He rounded the back of the vehicle and opened the backseat for me, smacking my ass as I slid in. "Time for that dessert you promised me" His eyes were glowing amber and his jaw ticked in anticipation.

"I guess we're past the getting-to-know-you phase, huh?" I pulled off my jacket and he slammed the door.

He yanked my boots off. I tugged on the zipper of my jeans and Viktor took care of the rest. "We most definitely are.

When you showed me that pretty little pussy on a video chat, you signed it over to me and now it's mine. Do you taste as good as you look, baby?" I licked my lips and didn't wait for a reply. I grabbed hold of her thighs and pushed them over my shoulders as I dove into her pussy with a flat tongue that ran from her ass to her clit. The moan she bellowed was desperate and encouraging and I finally felt at home.

Oh crap! "Let me remind you we're on the side of a highway and this is our first time together. Don't make me regret fantasizing about you as a gentleman." He laughed so loudly it made the car shake.

"I'll be a gentleman later, now I want to taste every part of you." And he did. Two hours of tasting, touching, connecting, and talking. Had we not stopped when we did the LAPD would have given us a ticket. As it was, we were just buckling back up and having one last kiss when they pulled up.

That man made a meal out of me that left me unconscious outside on the courthouse bench just before his meeting time. I insisted that his family's business was his own and that afterward if he wanted to debrief me on all the details, I'd be happy to listen. I was a distraction he couldn't afford.

I jerked awake unsure of my surroundings and took in the whirring of cars and bikes zooming down the road. The sun warmed my face in a way that Wisconsin never had. It felt, soft. It was the strangest feeling. Welcoming. Easy. Wisconsin summers were more, "Hey! I'm here. Come and get me before

I disappear again." This morning's sun was inviting me to relax and breathe and just let life happen.

I stood up and paced in front of the courthouse several times looking to see if they were coming down the stairs. I opened my email and answered anything important and saved the rest for later. Most of it was junk so I never paid too close attention to most of it. Rosie sent out her monthly schedule and implored us to find our own replacements if we were sick or needed to change her pristine calendar. My sister prodded me for more information about Viktor and insisted on daily details delivered by nine in the morning so she could enjoy them with her coffee and granola parfait, a staple for the past ten years.

It was almost Noon before I heard Viktor yelling at me from the top steps to come up. I ran all the way and stopped just before jumping into his arms. That would have been awkward with his parents standing there. His eyes were soft and a bit hazy. What did they say to him? Can he stay here?

He took my hand in his and threaded his fingers through mine reassuringly.

"So how did it go? Can you stay?" I was so unsure and fidgety that even his parents seemed uncomfortable.

"Ella, Love. These are my parents, Regina and Stephan." He pulled me in front of himself in solidarity so that I could be presented to his parents. "They've been not-so-patiently waiting to meet you." I looked up at him smirking at them.

I extended my hand to greet them when Regina pulled me tightly against her ample bosom followed by Stephan kissing both my cheeks proclaiming, "She's prettier than you told us."

The pink from my cheeks washed down my chest adding to the morning's warmth. They liked me. Though they should have reserved their opinions until we had some conversation. I could turn out to be a total embarrassment by the end of the day.

"It's such a pleasure meeting you. Viktor described you perfectly." His face glowed in appreciation and pride. "He is an exact replica of the two of you." DNA. It doesn't lie.

"You're too kind, dear. Let's go back to our home and we can have some cake and coffee. We have so much to share with you, and we want to hear everything about you." Regina wrapped her arm through mine and we walked down the steps to their car.

"Mom. Dad. Let me drop Ella's things at my apartment first and then we'll be over. Give us an hour. I'll bring Vodka. We have much to celebrate."

They hugged and patted his cheeks so lovingly it was hard to see him as an adult. Though once he closed the Towne car door sealing his mother inside, he turned his face to mine and he was no longer a sweet young man, he was a predator. His light brown eyes sparked gold as his brows pulled together. I could see his jaw working under his high cheekbones and there was no doubt whom he was stalking.

"Viktor. What are you doing?" I screamed as his stride increased until he swooped me up onto his shoulder, my head hanging dangerously close to his ass.

"Stealing you back to my car so I can fuck you silly."
Holy shit.

"You can't say that to me, I'm a fragile flower." I laughed hysterically smacking his ass as he speed-walked back to his car.

"Fragile flower, huh? We'll see how fragile you are when I have you spread out on my bed and my cock drilling into you." He flung me back over his shoulder and into the passenger seat and waggled his eyebrows. His mouth fused with mine torturing me with his tongue. Sucking and moaning his pleasure into mine whispering promises of pleasure.

He pulled back and buckled my seatbelt planting a soft whisper of a kiss that was as effective as his onslaught moments before. I was speechless and overwhelmed. What did I think would happen after traveling all night to a sex-starved man? Our foreplay started weeks ago and time wasn't our friend this weekend. Every moment had meaning and purpose. If I thought a few texts would lead to me flying across the country to be with a hot actor, I was delirious. It may, however, have delivered me to my future.

CHAPTER 10

VIKTOR

The ease that which we came together was so unexpected. Her smile was intoxicating and her ability to make everyone around her feel special and welcomed was purely magical. I could tell my parents were entranced by her, of course she would have had to be a serial killer for them not to love her. Not a chance that was happening.

I was thinking of all the ways I could fuck up this relationship when she interrupted me. I was always good at the physical side of things, but my commitment to any woman never stood the test of time. I always was evolving, moving, or not trusting someone. I had plenty of examples of why I shouldn't trust anyone, especially women. Ella, however, was something different altogether. Reliable. Trustworthy. Steadfast.

"Viktor?"

"Yes, sweetheart." I looked across the vehicle taking in her soft pink lips and incredibly blue eyes as she sipped her coffee.

"You didn't tell me how your meeting went. Will you be able to stay in the country?" Her lips trembled as the words left her mouth.

"For now. They agreed that this was a technicality and our family track record of being good tax-paying citizens will work in our favor, though they may put us on a parole-like program and track us if the judge deems it necessary. We won't have a final verdict until next month which is only two weeks away." I reached over and rubbed her shoulder squeezing it to give her all the reassurance I had at my disposal. Of course, what my lawyer said was contrary to everything I told her. The judge had political ties that put pressure on him to vet out any immigrant that didn't have pristine paperwork. I fucking hated politics and the politicians that abused the system for their benefit.

"That's great news. I'm so relieved. We should celebrate." Her eyes went wide and her tush bounced a little in her seat. "Where can we go for dinner? I haven't been out dancing in so long, let's do that too. Do you dance?" A free hand whipped around her head and in front of her face demonstrating her desire to move and I was all too happy to bump and grind her on the dance floor. We'll see how well she moves after I get her back to my apartment. We had less than an hour to reacquaint ourselves since this morning and making dinner plans wasn't a priority for me.

We entered my spacious apartment decorated in a variety of beige and tonal colors. I had no idea how to pick out a couch or what colors worked with one another so my agent referred me to an up-and-coming decorator to help me out. I gave her a list of my priorities and set her free; a comfortable couch for watching sports, relaxing colors, a king-sized bed with a down comforter, and round edges on all surfaces. I hated smacking into a sharp corner when I was drunk or half asleep. For a fraction of the cost of a high-end person, Emily delivered a perfect design. I've referred her to countless others and now she was on the hot list of decorators in L.A.

I ushered Ella into the apartment as she'd oo'd and ah'd at the view and the décor while I kept her moving toward my bedroom. I wasted no time stripping off my shirt, shoes, and socks.

"Strip," I commanded. She stopped abruptly and turned to face me, her mouth hanging open and her eyes looked confused. "Strip, now. Or I'll tear your clothes off for you." I took one step closer smelling her sweet soft perfume emanating from her clothes.

I stood there as she slowly unbuttoned her jeans sliding them seductively down her creamy-toned legs. Her panties dropped next laying in a pile between her legs. She looked at me cautiously. Why I wasn't sure. Approval? Insecurity?

"Baby you look edible." I encouraged her.

I wasn't waiting any longer. I closed the distance between us and pulled her hips tightly to my growing erection.

"Arms up." She obeyed and I grabbed the hem of her shirt and pulled it up over her head not so sweetly. Her arms fell to my shoulders as her fingers crept up my neck. I reached behind her and flicked the three hooks off her bra and let it fall to her elbows locking her arms in front of me. I couldn't have anything between us as I yanked it away and slid my hands down her curvy ass kneading them mercilessly.

"God, you're sexy." She moaned into my neck. I took that as a sign she wasn't put off by my alpha demeanor. Ella had no idea what I was capable of in bed. I wanted to do things for her that I'd never considered doing with anyone else. Things that involved trust and patience and understanding. I prayed at that moment that she was the person I was meant to be with. She had to be. I've been so patient and worked so hard for everything I've achieved and I wouldn't stop until she knew how important this relationship meant to me.

"Ella, you make me crazy when I'm with you. I want to show you how much you mean to me. Do you trust me?"

She stopped groping my body and I stopped kissing her waiting for her reply. Her eyes were cast downward and a nervousness shrouded her face like I hadn't seen before. Was she having second thoughts? We fooled around earlier so I wasn't sure why she was all of sudden so withdrawn. Did she decide she didn't want me? Didn't want like my alpha side? I needed to slow down and get to know her more before I blew it. Damn! I'm always too full-on. When would I learn?

"Viktor." I felt her heart beating along mine, fast and unsure. "I've never been so sure about someone before. I just think we shouldn't push too hard this first weekend. If we're right together, then we have more opportunities to go deeper into everything."

Fucking hell, she was right, but more importantly, she didn't say no. We wanted the same things though she was more conscientious of pacing ourselves. Her wisdom would serve us both well as we maneuvered our careers and the logistics of our lives together.

I slid both my hands under her jaw tilting her face so her lips perfectly fit over mine. "You're incredible." I licked her upper lip softly. Slowly. "How did I get so lucky to find you?" I slid my tongue along hers sucking it in my mouth more deeply. God. I couldn't get enough of her.

Her hands smoothed the lock of hair that fell over my brow. Like an angel, she massaged her fingers over my head and down my neck releasing the remaining stress I held from earlier that day. I was busy nuzzling her jaw and neck while she was busy snaking her capable hands down my pecs, over my abdominal crevices, and into the waistband of my jeans. *Clever girl.*

"Take me, Vik. I've waited too long not to have you inside me." We could slow down after I had her.

Her whispered commands left no confusion as to what she wanted and what I had planned for her. I let her fondle my cock as I dipped my head to the hard-pointed nub of her left breast. The sounds she emitted would be etched into my mind to be played back over and over again. My pants and underwear were already halfway down my thighs when she stepped on the crotch crushing them to the floor.

Time was not on our side and if we could have languidly spent this weekend learning about each other's bodies, we would have. Sadly, that was not the case so I grabbed both her ass cheeks and threw her to the bed. Her laugh was infectious and I joined her like we just shared a great joke. She was nervous and so was I. I wanted to make our first time together so good. So memorable. But when she tried to crawl up the bed I grabbed her thighs and pulled her back down as I fell to my knees and stared at my prize.

"It's been so long, Vik." I sucked her clit fingered her opening getting her ready for me. I knew I had a big cock and I didn't want to hurt so I massaged her opening for another minute before her hips bucked up against my face screaming, "Yes, yes, yes!" My sick mind wanted to explore more of her essence and I would have my wish later tonight without fail but my dick was ready to launch into her now.

"Move up to the pillows, darling. I want to make this special for you." Her eyebrows raised as she touched her fingertips to her mouth in anticipation. "Reach between your legs and taste yourself. Have you ever done that?" I was pushing her, I knew it. I needed to know how dirty my girl would allow herself to be, and when she did, I almost blew my load.

"Fuck, El. You're so hot. Did you like it?" She gave me a naughty little girl smile like her hand was caught in the cookie jar and nodded licking her fingers again. Damn! I reached over to my nightstand and grabbed a couple of condoms, wasting no time ripping one open and sliding it onto my shaft. All the rumors about Ukrainians and big cocks were true for me and my dirty girl was going to be pleasantly stretched wide.

I let her watch me palm my sack allowing her to enjoy all my assets. She licked her lips and moaned, "So big." I grinned back, "All for you baby. All for you."

I kneed her legs open then used my hands to push them wider. "Let me in, El," I said as I pressed my throbbing head quickly and deeply into her wetness. The gasps we both expelled said it all. Our eyes locked and I felt a spiritual connection so deep that our souls seemed to merge. I was hers and she was mine and the world no longer existed. I moved slowly giving her time to adjust to my girth moving faster when she gripped my shoulders.

"Please, Viktor. Faster, please. I need…" Her voice fell away as her back arched in approval. I moved her legs over my shoulders and lifted her ass clear off the mattress giving myself the deepest penetration I had ever had and was rewarded when we came together. Explosive. Soulful. Mind-blowing sex that left me speechless and profoundly sated.

"What. The hell. Was that?" She said through gulps of air. "I've been abducted and returned to earth a new woman." I rolled off her pulling her alongside me, holding her like a lifeline. Minutes went by and I still hadn't answered her. I was in awe.

"Viktor. Are you okay?" She stroked my arm wrapped around her breast. I didn't want this moment to end. I needed more time.

"Yeah. That was…other-worldly sex." I fell to my back unable to think clearly. What do you say to a woman that has just given you the single most incredible moments of your life? "Wow! That was awesome. You're incredible. I think I love you." Oh my God, I think I do love her. Can I say that now? No. Don't rush it. She literally said not to rush things. But…

"Exactly. You have an incredibly magical schlong. I had no idea sex could be like that. Again, I say, where did you come from and how was I lucky enough to find you?" She slid her fingers through my own and kissed the back of my hand. It was a moment of reckoning. We were made for each other. Now we had to find a way to stay with each other.

CHAPTER 11

ELLA

How do you say no to a guy that checks every box on your perfect-man list? We met his parents back at their home, albeit later than planned, and he wanted me to cook with his mom. He said it would be a great way for the two of us to get to know each other better, but it felt a little contrived.

"Really, Viktor. I'm not a good cook, and I just met her. What will we even talk about?" I pleaded my case.

Of course, he laughed at my feeble excuses. He assumed I was gregarious and open to such things. I was socially inept, hence my lack of male companionship. I used my profession as a façade to relate to people. It wasn't that I was particularly shy, it was that I sucked with small talk. Give me a beefy topic with lots of gooey details and I was okay, anything but trite conversation.

I stuck out my lower lip pouting, "Fine. Only because I came all this way, but you have to stay in the kitchen until I'm comfortable." My finger tapping his taut chest was designed to emphasize my point but his laughter mocked me.

"You are so adorable when you're mad." He picked me up by my ass and wrapped my legs around his waist. "I'll protect you from my mama." His warm tongue outlined my lips and then sank deep into my mouth. His kisses were pornographic and we were right outside their front door. I pulled my legs down pushing away from his chest as I heard the front door unlocking.

"You, are incorrigible." He snickered and we both turned to greet them.

Shrieks of joy came from behind the sapphire blue wood door. Both his parents stood there smiling and swinging their arms toward the inside of their home seemingly desperate for us to get inside.

"*Dorohoi*! Where have you been? We've been waiting for you. Come, coffee is ready. We eat." His parents ushered us into their small but homey kitchen. A small wooden table for two was now transformed into four and pulled away from the wall. White aluminum blinds hung over the sink window and door wall leading to a quaint patio in the backyard. Delicate lace draped over the front of the blinds softening their harsh edges. Tiny blossoms dotted the worn wallpaper and a large wooden cross hung under a ticking clock. These are religious people and I'm afraid I might let loose an expletive that would embarrass me. I don't swear all the time though I've been known to drop an F-bomb when provoked. My anxiety ratcheted up another notch. All I wanted to do was support Viktor, not look like a circus clown to his parents.

Like a mind reader, Viktor set the tone for our visit today.

"Mama. Papa. Thank you so much for meeting Ella. She has come to mean so much to me. Don't smother her. I want her to stick around." He smiled and winked pulling out a chair for me to sit on. He pulled his chair closer allowing his strength to comfort me. I smiled and hoped that I was presenting myself well.

"You have a lovely home, Mrs. Zolofa. Thank you so much for having me over. Can I help with anything?" I wasn't a complete failure as a guest. I was taught how to behave in polite company. Time to put those skills to the test.

"Thank you *doroghoia*, but I've got it." She turned and walked the few steps to the counter where she transferred a tea tray of cookies, sugar, cream, and coffee. Beautiful porcelain cups with a similar flower as the wallpaper were filled with a thick liquid resembling malted coffee. I whispered to Viktor.

"Doroghoia?" I ruffled my brows.

"Sweetheart." He winked again.

My mouth rounded to an O as he patted his knee. He responded with his large palm running up the length of my thigh sending tingles all over my body and doing that little smirk thing he does when he's mocking me. How the hell was I supposed to know Ukrainian? I needed to get myself a translator app, fast.

Our chat at the table lasted almost an hour as we covered where I came from, who my parents are, and what they do, all the way through college, finishing with my current occupation. The interrogation ended with Viktor pushing back from the table and clapping his hand together once.

"Let's cook!" He commanded.

As we carried our dishes to the sink, Regina put away the cookies and Stephan pulled out a large pan and stockpot. This family was a well-oiled machine when it came to cooking. Everyone had a job, and it looked like Viktor was the shopper gathering all the veggies from around the kitchen, and a large bottle of oil from the pantry.

I felt pretty useless since I didn't have a clue as to what we were making so I sat at the counter bar and watched the choreography play out. Stephan pulled out several pounds of ground pork and a package of dinner rolls and mozzarella cheese and with each ingredient after that, I became more and more confused as to what we were making.

I bumped shoulders with Vik and whispered, "What are we making?" The smile on his face pulled from ear to ear. "You haven't heard of piroshki?" He pulled me to his side and kissed my forehead feeling sorry for me.

"So far it looks like we're making hot pockets." His eyes may have rolled a little.

"No, no, no. piroshki is decidedly Ukrainian unless you're Polish, then it's pierogi." Both Vik and his dad were shaking their heads and swishing their pointy fingers back and forth, not allowing for any further conversation. *Whatever.*

Not wanting to make this uncomfortable, I conceded and gave a little bow. "It seems we are at an impasse as to who is responsible for these delicious treats, but I'm sure the rest of us Americans are happy to have them on our tables."

Regina humpfed her reply. "Now only if America could appreciate industrious people that bring diverse cultures together to make a better country." She worked the meat with spices in a big stainless-steel bowl while the guys decided it was a good time to take their leave. Viktor blew me a kiss and rolled his eyes at his parents. Regina pointed to the cast iron pan and olive oil, "Pour a couple of tablespoons into the pan and turn the heat to six. We will fry them soon." I nodded and stepped around the counter to do her bidding.

"When I have more time, I like to make a sweet dough to wrap around each piroshki but sometimes I cheat and use these rolls. I've already prepped them so I'll need you to flatten them into circles so we can stuff them." Why did this feel like a test? It should have been flub-proof although we were talking about me in the kitchen, and well, my circles looked more like trapezoids.

I showed one to her for approval and her tummy jumped and her smile pulled up to one side. Her kindness shone through by not making me feel like an idiot when she pressed the rolls together with her left hand resembling an L and her right fingers like a backward L. She curled her fingers and manipulated the dough into a perfect circle in one try. I was so embarrassed at how easy she made it look that I worked really hard on the next ones to redeem myself.

"Dis good." She proclaimed and took a sip of water. "You like to cook?" She kept her hands busy and chopped the onions and carrots like Edward Scissorhands, so fast and precise. It was amazing how comfortable she was in the kitchen. I hoped Viktor didn't have that same expectation.

She directed me back to the pan and I turned on the burners while she stuffed a half dozen meat pies together. It was easier speaking with her while my back was to hers. Her stare could be intimidating, though I don't think she was trying to make me feel uncomfortable. Still, she drilled me for answers about my life.

"I do like to cook when I have the time. The hours I keep prohibit me from making good home-cooked meals very often. It seems easier to make a deli or tuna sandwich for lunch or grab a bowl of soup from the hospital cafeteria." I set the first piroshki in the oil and waited for my next direction. I flipped them checking to be sure they were lightly browned and then asked, "Would you like to check these? I think they're done." I stepped away from the stove and handed her the spatula. She pushed her finger lightly onto the dough and flipped them back pushing again.

"Perfect. Good job, Ella." Wonderful. I get a gold star for not burning dinner. At least I passed that test. I can't imagine what she'll have me do next. "Next, salad." She pushed one of each vegetable across the counter entrusting me to cut the pieces evenly without taking off my finger. It was a fifty-fifty craps shoot.

I focused intently on making my pieces small and even. In the process, I found myself taking control of the conversation. It was my turn to learn more about her family and hoped I'd collect some pearls from Viktor's childhood. There were so many gaps in his story I'd like to undercover, and I'm sure if we had known each other longer those holes may have been filled, but I kept forgetting we just met a few weeks ago. My zeal to know everything about him consumed me and it also scared me. I never wanted to know all the details about any other guy I liked. What did I care if his family liked piroshki? Or if he spent a lot of time with his parents? This was a tight-knit family with a strong hold on keeping it that way while honoring their culture. This was something I'd have to think about. His parents had to be his number one concern. Where would that leave me? Would I ever have a chance to be in that number one spot? I would never make him choose or become a wedge in their relationship.

I cleared my throat keeping my tone light, "So, Regina. Tell me about Viktor when he was a boy. Was he always into mischief? Did he play sports?" I smiled thinking of him running in circles on a soccer field.

"Oh, that boy was always in trouble. Climbing trees, chasing goats, and leaving the gate open so the dog always ran free." We both laughed at the images of all those boyish things. "But he was a good boy. Always with good manners and take care of his sister." Sister? I thought he was an only child.

I pursed my lips thinking back to all the conversations we had since I met him and I'm sure he never said anything about a sister. "I'm sorry, Viktor never mentioned he has a sister. Where does she live?"

She put down the spatula and stepped back from the counter. She stretched out her arm to open the refrigerator and pulled out butter and sour cream all without a single word. The pain in her face sent chills down my spine. I regretted even asking. After a moment she wiped her weeping eyes with the back of her hand. It was hard to know if it was from the onions or my inquiry. When she lifted her chin I instantly knew it was my question.

"I'm so sorry, Regina. I didn't mean to make you cry. Forget I even asked." I put my head down and forced myself to finish my task without opening up my big mouth again.

Calloused hands settled on top of mine and my eyes raised to lock with hers. We looked deeply into each other's eyes longer than was comfortable until she pressed her lips tightly together.

"It's not your fault you don't know anything about her. It's my stupid son that left that part of his life out when telling you about his family." We both smirked at that statement. "Irina passed away of pneumonia at three years old. We left Ukraine six months later. We needed a new beginning and the politics were, eh, getting worse."

"Oh, Regina!" I gasped. "How tragic for you all." I bowed my head in despair for her pain. What else could I do?

She patted my hands and brought and turned back to the frying pan. She mechanically continued to prepare the meal sharing bits and pieces of Irina's tale. "She was born prematurely leaving her with weak lungs. We did our best to help her with medicine but they were hard to get. Viktor pushed her buggy around the yard dancing and singing to keep her entertained so that I could tend to the house. He was the best big brother." She sniffled and plated the food from the paper towels they had been draining on. "We hoped she would outgrow her condition except that winter was especially cold and she couldn't get enough air. We rushed her to the hospital but we didn't have a car, only the bus, and we were too late to help her. Shortly after we arrived she gasped her last breath with the word Viktor on her lips."

I was stunned. Never in my life did I see that coming. No wonder he couldn't speak her name. I put down my knife and ran around the counter and took Regina into my arms. "You poor woman. I'm so sorry for your loss, and for your whole family's loss. I'm an emergency nurse and every time a child passes it's as though a piece of your heart is torn out. I can't even imagine how you can carry on after that." We held each other and cried for several minutes doing our best to settle our tears and our hearts. That was when Viktor chose to come back into the kitchen.

"Well, look at you two bonding like sisters." His smooth swagger faltered as our red eyes turned toward his. "What's going on? Is something wrong?"

Regina turned back towards the pan as she waved us off. Viktor opened the patio door, his hand at the small of my back, and guided me to a set of chairs that looked out over the valley. He turned his chair to face mine and our knees touched. The feel of his hands coming up to my red cheeks to wipe the remaining tears comforted me after such an incredible story. I wasn't sure if I wanted to be sorry for him or beat him over the head for leaving that giant detail out of our conversations.

"Baby, what happened in there?" His breath brushed over my face. "Do I need to beat my mother up?" He kissed me softly. I realized now how much he used humor to distract me from what he really felt.

"I think I'd rather beat you up." I slapped his chest not so playfully.

"Hey, what did I do?"

"It's not what you did, but what you didn't do. You never in all our conversations mentioned you had a sister. A sister whom you doted on." His face morphed into a painful squeeze. I wanted to hold him and tell him how terrible I felt about the circumstances of her passing, but my pride was still intact. "Why didn't you tell me? I could have handled it. I deal with death every day."

He scrubbed his face with both hands pulling them to the back of his neck. His mesmerizing arms were displayed so perfectly that I wanted to forget what we were fighting about and crawl into them. He has a way of making me feel safe, just like my sister. My head snapped back to reality and I fell back into the chair.

"Ella, please believe me that I never meant to hurt you. Irina was a small but powerful memory that I've never shared with anyone. We were, are, starting to get to really know each other and I had to know that I could trust you with such a fragile piece of my heart and my past. Did you know that she died saying my name? I mean, how the hell does a kid move forward after hearing and seeing that? I stopped speaking for six months. My parents were out of their minds about what to do with me. They petitioned for visas, packed up their home, said goodbye to their family and friends, and moved to a foreign land only knowing very little English. It was another trauma I had to endure and get over quickly. The loss of my sister faded since we had to figure out our new lives. To this day, we almost never bring up her name."

Like his mother, I flung myself into his arms and kissed his mouth. I snuggled deeper into his chest and hoped that my love and forgiveness would permeate his soul. He palmed the back of my head and tucked me under his chin stroking my hair and whispering his apology over and over again. We sat like that for quite a while until his dad poked his head out of the screen door, "Dinner is ready when you are."

My snot was rubbed into his skin and I laughed at the grossness of it. "You're going to need to clean up before dinner. I left a mess all over you."

"Don't worry beautiful. I'm going to leave a mess all over you later."

CHAPTER 12

VIKTOR

E**l was angry. Really angry. This was the first time we argued and the thought of her walking away from me was worse than the feeling of being kicked out of the country. They could send me away, but she was coming with me. She just didn't know it yet.

I hadn't thought about Irina in a few years. She was part of my past and probably the reason I don't trust anyone. They leave you when you trust them. They extract what they want and then rip your heart out when you need them the most. Two months after we arrived in California, my parents were very upset at my tantrums. Home, church, and even at school. Nothing in particular would trigger me though after several sessions with the school social worker, she identified my condition as PTSD. As an adult, I knew it was a condition from something traumatic happening, but when you're six years old you don't have the words or the perspective needed to explain your situation. Losing my sister, then immediately moving, left me floundering without a compass. My parents were so busy getting our new home set up and starting their new jobs that I spent most of my time in front of a television playing video games. Those were easy to control, my life wasn't. Now how do I simplify all this for Ella? She deserves to know the truth. The whole truth. Though not all of it tonight.

She tried to slip off my lap but I banded my arms around her waist and whispered over her shoulder, "I'm sorry I didn't tell you about, Irina. There are so many layers to this story and I didn't want to dump it on you. I wanted our time together to be fun. Interesting. Easy. Please forgive me. I'll give you all the details, just not right now." My hand ran up her back to rest on the nape of her neck massaging the stress away from the day.

She slumped back into me with a deep sigh. "I forgive you. I keep forgetting we only met a few weeks ago. It feels like so much longer. And, of course, your sister's passing is something very personal and private. You've told me so many deep things about you I figured, you know, that it would have come up already."

Her arms lifted and snaked around the back of my head to pull me down to her face. The turn of her head brought her soft pink lips closer and I took what I needed to put myself at ease. Her tongue pushed into my mouth and danced with my own. She had a way of discharging my anxieties like a pill for pain. Good thing she chose nursing as her profession. She was my new drug of choice.

Hesitantly I pulled back wishing we had more time, "Come on, baby. My parents are waiting on us, again." She swatted my chest as I pushed her off my knees.

"You're the reason we're always late, buddy. Greedy hands and seductive whispers will get you everything." We laughed as I opened the patio door getting one last ass cheek palmed in my hand. Her eye roll was precious.

Two hours later when dinner was finished, an embarrassing round of family photo fun began. We managed to slide into my car and made our way back to my apartment. Ella had never been to Cali so on a whim I decided to make a scenic stop.

"Close your eyes," I commanded.

"Why?"

"Please do it. Humor me," I jeered.

"Fine," she said with disgust.

I came around the final curve of the Mulholland Highway and pulled into the parking lot in the foothills of Mt. Lee.

"Keep your eyes closed. I'm coming around to get you." I sure hope she listened to me. I wanted to see her expression when she saw my surprise.

I opened her door sliding my hand deliberately over her breast and she giggled as I unbuckled her seatbelt. "Smooth, Viktor."

"Doing my best, sweetheart."

I took her hand and carefully led her to the scrub that lined the hiking trail. She shuffled her feet the whole way not trusting that I'd keep her out of danger. I'm going to have to fix that. I scooped her up in my arms and marched her up the trail as she whooped and hollered to put her down. She found my head and wrapped her hands around my neck pulling me closer as her arms slid over my shoulders. That was better.

"Put me down, Viktor. What the hell? Where are you taking me? You'd better not be kidnapping me right now. People know I'm here!" And with that, I dropped her to her feet. She was becoming agitated and people started looking our way. I didn't need that kind of trouble.

Keeping her close to my chest I spoke softly and confidently, "Settle yourself down and keep those eyes shut we're almost there." Five more steps and we had arrived.

"Now. When I say 'three' you open your eyes. Okay?"

"Okay." She bounced from foot to foot like a little girl. *This was going to be amazing.*

"One, two, two-and-half, two-and-three quarters…THREE!"

Her eyes flung open and within nanoseconds, they widened showing me her long lashes and stunning turquoise eyes.

Her hands smacked her gaping mouth and jumped up and down, "The Hollywood Sign! OMG! I can't believe it." She quickly turned to me and grabbed my shirt. "You're taking me up there, right? I want to touch it." Two more spins around in a circle and she settled her hands into tiny claps in front of her ample chest. Mission accomplished.

"So, you like my surprise?" I grinned and banded my arms around her waist pulling her back to my chest.

"I do. I really, really do."

"To answer your question, no, we will not be going up there to touch it. It's against the law. We can, however, hike up close to it and take some pictures if you'd like. Maybe fool around a little?" Even though the sun was setting and visitors were heading back to their cars I couldn't afford to get caught screwing around with my girl on a hillside. One unaccounted photo from a fan could complicate my immigration status and create a media frenzy, not to mention Ella's life could also be in jeopardy.

I threaded my fingers through hers and pulled her behind me as I took the trail up the foothills as the sun dropped another few degrees. The air was clear for a change, and the sweet smell of lavender and soil filled floated up my nostrils. We walked in silence passing a few teenagers, one of whom stopped and pulled on his friend's shirt and pointed at me. Busted. I knew it would happen. It happened more and more lately, and I hated it. My fame was growing, and all I wanted was to be invisible so I could be with my woman without my image being pimped out on the internet.

The kids moved on and as we crested the top of one of the lower hills and looked straight up. Our ascent ended here since we weren't mountain climbing to touch the letters. Ella's in shape. She barely had time to catch her breath though once we stopped, she leaned into my chest and hugged me tightly. I bent to kiss her head and took in a big breath of her peach-smelling shampoo. Proving this girl was, in fact, peaches and cream, making that my new favorite treat.

"Having fun, baby?" I hummed into her ear.

"Mmm," she hummed back, her face nuzzled under my chin, "The best."

I took out my phone and opened the camera to change into selfie mode.

"Are you ready for your first photo shoot with a leading man in an upcoming film?" My eyebrows waggled and I pulled her back to my chest. "Any and all photos are the property of us. They are our superpower and cannot be shared with anyone else." I have no idea why my silly legalese poured from my lips except she needed a gentle reminder of what these pictures are really worth to the paparazzi. I'm an ass. I needed to shut up. "Seriously. Let's have some fun."

She turned abruptly in my arms taking my face in her hands. Her eyebrows pulled tight and a wry smile turned her lips into a grimace.

"Listen, Mr. Badass Hollywood superstar, I don't want my picture in a magazine. I don't want my life smeared across a title banner. You are the only thing I want. Only you. The rest of the world can fuck itself. Do you understand my terms of engagement?"

My face pushed through her hands until my mouth was on hers pressing her lips open and exploring hers deeply. The little moans that resonated in my mouth went straight to my cock. I can't believe I found the one woman who is the real deal. Focused only on me and not what was in it for her. I grabbed her round ass and pulled her into my thickening shaft. Her hands dove into my hair and pulled at the short hair above. I never knew how turned on that made me feel but I wanted that feeling forever.

I pulled back to look into her eyes that now resembled lapis lazuli. Stunning. "I accept your terms and raise you one higher. I want, no, need you to trust me when I ask you to only say, 'no comment,' should you be approached. We need to be strong together and I want to protect you as much as I can. Okay."

She stared me down I presumed to see how serious I was, and when the corners of her mouth tipped up, I knew I could trust her implicitly. I had to believe that for my peace of mind and hers.

"I'm calling," our poker talk continued. "I won't speak to anyone without your prior approval. I would never intentionally cause you harm and in turn, cause me harm. I'm a simple woman, Viktor. I don't have an agenda with you or anyone else. I want honesty and I truly believe you'll be honest with me, always." She pulled my face again to place delicate kisses on each corner of my mouth and then a longer kiss in the middle. It was a promise and I would take it to the bank.

"I know you wouldn't. Enough of this. Picture time!"

I spun her around and reset the camera to take a series of three shots on a timer photo booth style. The goofy pictures were hysterical and I wanted more. With the timer set again, and my arm stretched out as far as it would go, I used my other hand to pull her closer. This kiss would leave an indelible mark on her in a way I wanted to be recorded forever.

The sun had set and the air became too cool to hang out any longer, so I suggested we get going. I sat down on a rock to retie my shoe when El decided now would be a good time to be a monkey and climbed onto my back.

"Be a good caveman and carry me down the hill." She chuckled into my shoulder.

I threw my head back and gave her my best gorilla impersonation that had her laughing so hard she was choking me. We made it back to the car after nearly tumbling down the last slope, El sliding off my back before I nose-dived into a cactus. My director wouldn't appreciate that next week. This whole actor gig made it almost impossible to have fun for fear of maiming myself. I should investigate a new career. I mean, I had been studying to go into public health and only had one year left for my degree. *Hmm?*

"You're thinking." She was too perceptive. I took her hand again and led her over to the passenger side of the car with my other hand guiding her hip.

"You're too smart." I tucked her into her seat and kissed her tit through the fabric pulling her nub through the material.

"Jesus, Vik. Give a girl a warning." He looked like the devil he really was.

"Yeah. I am pretty smart. So, what's up?" Her insistence was endearing except me finishing my degree was something I wasn't ready to commit to and I didn't want to get her hopes up.

I made my way around the back of the car and opened my door when I saw her studying my face. I'm not sure what I looked like but she was on to me and I needed a response that would ease her mind.

"I'm tossing around some ideas of what the future may hold." I couldn't look at her anymore without blurting out my ideas. I buckled up and started the car only turning towards her when I backed up to leave.

"The future, huh? Would that future include an ER nurse from Wisconsin?" She bit her lip and my spine tingled thinking about the last time she did that.

"You better stop looking at me like that or I'll pull this car over and spank that fine ass of yours." Her jaw dropped and her hands smacked her chest. "That's right. I mean it young lady." We laughed so much that she didn't bring up the topic again. A brief reprieve for me, I'm sure. Twenty minutes later we made it back to my apartment and the rest of the evening we spent imprinting ourselves onto each other. Hands, hips, tits, ass, lips, and everything in between. We only had one more day and I wasn't sure when we'd see each other again. I wanted to remember every inch of her. I wasn't sure what the future held for us though if I had my way, we would be in the same bed every night, whispering our dreams and desires under the covers, me deep inside her planting my seed, and growing a family.

CHAPTER 13

ELLA

When I finally rolled my sore body onto my side, I was comforted knowing that I was still alive. Last night was the most heavenly athletic evening of my life, and I was a decorated swimmer. Viktor had moves only porn stars could execute and let me tell you, I might need to change my profession now that I've tried them. That man was gifted and I felt greedy for more. I wanted him, I needed him. That feeling of loneliness and aloneness lifted from my head and heart. I didn't want to feel that way ever again and it seemed as though he may feel the same way.

    I managed to get my feet on the floor and took in my first full breath of the day only to inhale the glorious smell of coffee, the elixir of life. I slipped on one of his t-shirts sitting on a chair in the corner. I followed the nutty aroma into the kitchen and found my man making eggs shirtless and sexy as fuck in one of his European modal thongs. My hunger for food fought with my hunger to experience his body again and when he saw me licking my lips, he decided for me. The hissing of gas was extinguished as he walked to the other side of the island and stopped inches from where I stood.

"Morning, beautiful." His breath was minty and his body oozed sex appeal. He watched me carefully. I'd never seen irises change so deeply as his did. My breath hitched at the intensity of his stare and my hands reached for his pecs without thinking. The smooth-toned skin turned to gooseflesh under my touch showing signs of appreciation as I lightly brushed my palms from his nipples to his shoulders.

"Good morning, my sexy hot boyfriend. I'm not sure what I'm hungrier for, you or those eggs." My cheeks flushed at my brazenness and given all the naughty things we did to each other last night I shouldn't be embarrassed. He didn't move an inch letting me explore his body without interruption. I stepped forward pressing my breasts against his abs tracing the long vein from his shoulder down to his elbow watching the way it flexed and pulsed along the way. I looked lovingly at his lips that hovered over mine but still, he wouldn't move.

"Kiss me, Viktor," I pleaded in a whisper.

He pulled on my bottom lip sucking it into his mouth possessively. My hands pushed into his hair imploring him to take more.

"You are so fucking sexy." His tongue plunged into my mouth sucking and twisting around my own. It was wet and sloppy and full of desire. "I swear I could eat you alive." First my mouth, then my neck, and when he bent to take my needy breast into his mouth, I moaned my pleasure. He bent down and drove his shoulder into my hips and lifted me into a fireman's carry as if I didn't weigh a thing. I screamed and giggled and smacked his taunt ass as he carried me back to the bedroom muttering something in Ukrainian. It was when he smacked my ass so hard that I knew I was going to be breakfast.

I'd learned that when Viktor makes a decision there is no stopping him. He whipped me off his shoulder and set me on the end of his bed. "Don't move." His stare was serious and when he pointed his finger at me to stay, he reminded me of what my father did when he was angry.

I sat very still concerned about what I said or did that upset him.

He came back from the bathroom with an evil gleam in his eyes that implied I was a naughty girl that needed a lesson.

"Did I do something wrong? Are you mad at me?" I think this was the reason we were given cuticles so that we had something to bite when we were nervous. He diverted his course to the closet to retrieve a foam wedge and motioned for me to push myself up to the middle of the bed. The casualness in his stride reeked of confidence and control that my insides vibrated hysterically.

"Mad at you? Why would I be mad at you?" His eyebrows scrunched while he pulled the blankets out of the way.

"You pointed your finger at me like I was a naughty girl. My dad pointed his finger at me when he was mad." My pout was enough to have him crawl up my legs and straddle me.

"Unless you plan to call me daddy, please don't associate me pointing a finger at you as your father reprimanding you. I was only pointing out that I didn't want you to move from that spot." His smile reassured me, although calling him daddy did have its allure. He pushed back and grabbed the wedge again. "Lift your legs up to your shoulders." I loved it when he commanded me in a whisper to do dirty things, it made me feel desired. He placed the wedge so that my lower half folded over my chest without me having to hold them there and proceeded to kiss my inner thighs slowly and seductively from my knees to my wet core.

"God, Viktor! You are a wicked man." I screamed.

"Quiet. I'm having my breakfast." The growl he made gave my belly butterflies. He was an animal when he took me, not that I was complaining. His magical tongue found my wanting clit and circled it slowly over and over pulling it with the perfect amount of suction to bring me over the edge. I arched and bucked as he continued to lap up all my juices moaning at how much he loved my pussy. The man had skills and I was happy to provide him a sense of accomplishment.

"Oh. My. God. You're amazing." I screamed through my hands. I had never had a man know what to do to get me off without having to create a fantasy in my head, let alone have an arsenal of techniques to do it efficiently and effectively. I bet with a little time he could train me and my pussy to come on demand. He was just that good.

"Maybe I do have the perfect pussy to love." His eyes locked onto mine and the air stilled. That word held so much power now and for our future together.

In a flash, he had his thong off and was back straddling my chest. The way he precariously pulled off the shirt I was wearing while dangling his rock-hard cock over my mouth was intoxicating. The drop of precum sliding off the tip and falling across my cheek had my head turning to have my own breakfast. I strained to lick his cock as he mocked me.

"Are you hungry, baby?" He grabbed his shaft pulling hard several times before nudging himself closer. "Open." He commanded. His thick-veined member made my mouth water and especially as he tapped it on my tongue with a pulse that matched my heartbeat. *God, he was kinky.* He pushed himself deeper into my mouth and I took him back the way he liked it. The sounds it made were sick and dissonate but resonated so well within me. I wanted him in ways I never knew existed before this weekend. I didn't know I had a kinky side, but Viktor knew. How? I'll never know.

A minute or two later he pulled his shaft from my throat and lifted his leg back over me making his way to the end of the bed. He stared at me with an intensity that I'd come to crave. My legs were above my shoulders and my pussy on full display, all he had to do was push into me. To drive his cock deeper than he ever had.

"Ella. You are so incredibly beautiful and open to new experiences. I hope you'll like this next one." He mounted the bed sliding his strong hand up and down his shaft while his other pressed the back of my thigh deeper into my shoulder. My ass was higher than my head when he pressed into my pussy. From this angle, I saw stars and felt a white-hot twinge of ecstasy I'd only dreamt about. He pressed himself so quickly and deeply I burst into tears.

"Oh, my God. Viktor. More. There. More." I couldn't breathe and couldn't think straight. The euphoria of him pounding me so deeply and precisely had me gasping for air. His body was taught and sweaty and so focused on driving into me over and over again that he didn't see how epic this moment was for me. I felt transformed as he pressed his thumb onto my clit and circled until I burst into a million tiny specs of light. It was at that moment that he looked up and captured the utter bliss he created in me. My uterus clenched over and over again milking him of his orgasm and I knew by the immense reaction in both of us that we were meant to be together forever.

"Fuck, fuck, oh my God, El. Fuck!" Viktor continued to pump me until he collapsed onto my thighs, his breath jerky and raspy from his exertions. He slowly pulled himself out of me and held my legs while he removed the wedge. He set them down and gently slid next to me tugging me onto his chest while we held each pondering what was to come next.

VIKTOR

There were no words to describe the feelings this woman created in me. I am an actor and still, I couldn't find the right words to explain the series of emotions coursing through my mind and body. Otherworldly? Transformative? Holy? All of those and more. We didn't need words now, we needed touch and tenderness. That was our language. I gathered both her hands and laid them on my heart and shared my truth with her.

"I can't tell you what it meant to me to have you fly out this weekend. You could have begged off as too busy, or it was too much too soon, but you didn't. You made yourself available to me regardless of the circumstances and I'll never forget it,

El. I'm pretty sure my immigration situation will resolve itself soon but if I had to go…" I wouldn't allow myself to go there. It couldn't happen and I wouldn't let it happen. "Enough of that, have you ever been to the Pacific Ocean."

I rubbed her belly and began to tickle her up to her armpits. Her laughter was infectious as she swatted at me squealing loudly. I pushed up to my elbow keeping her legs across mine dragging my fingers over her calves and feet unconsciously.

She laughed. "No, I haven't. Do you think we'll see Rob Lowe or Denzel Washington? They're hot." Her lips pressed together.

"So, you like older men, huh? Experienced men, that work hard and are versatile?" She nodded silently. "So, what you're saying is, men that look like me? Have a reputation like me, but are thirty years older than you?" I tickled her feet.

"Maybe." She laughed raucously.

"You're a stinker." I pulled her up to my chest and kissed her hard." I'll tell you what, stick around long enough and we'll be both thirty years older."

Oh shit! Did I suggest we spend our lives together? There I went again. Now I'm skipping decades instead of months!

"Did I freak you out? I think I freaked myself out right now. Don't answer that. Come on," I said shoving her to her feet. "Let's get cleaned up and I'll take you to breakfast and then the beach. Maybe I'll say and do more stupid things to freak you out."

While she showered, I threw some towels, sunscreen, and hats in a bag. I knew a place where we could rent an umbrella and enjoy the whole day relaxing. I took my turn in the shower and she found her swimsuit and sunglasses and were out the door within thirty minutes. If only she hadn't worn that sexy sundress, I could have kept my hands off her during the ride over.

Our day was filled with walks in the sand, splashing each other like children, and sharing funny work stories and dreams of our futures. Everything and anything that didn't speak of love, and a future together. Every hour was like a day together. We knew so much and so little that anyone looking at us would think, "They must have been together for years." *If only.*

We changed back into our street clothes and found a quaint bistro for a light dinner. Seagulls squawked overhead as the sun fell from the sky in a measured rhythm. We drank red wine and listened to a jazz trio croon songs of pained love and weathered hearts. I felt every note.

"You have a terrible poker face, Vik." She reached out and brushed my tanned cheek with her knuckles.

"Yeah, so I've been told."

"I know what you're thinking." She cupped my chin and stood up to press her lips lightly to mine.

"You do?" I threaded my fingers through her tresses and pulled her in for a fuller kiss.

"Yes. You want the world to fade away leaving the two of us alone to enjoy each other." She sat back and sipped again.

"Exactly. You should consider mind reading. You have an uncanny way of reading people, especially me." My glass was empty and I signaled to the waiter to bring our check.

"It's been a perfect day. Thank you for suggesting this. Wisconsin isn't known for its beaches and perfectly bronzed tans." She pulled her purse onto her lap and dug around for something until she showed me her prize, lip gloss. Why she bothered, I have no idea. I was going to kiss it off anyway.

"I'm the one who should be thanking you. You saved my ass by being a true friend. I really couldn't have gotten through this immigration thing without you even if I won't have an answer for a few weeks." Her smile was heartfelt and lifted my spirits immensely.

The waiter brought the bill and I slapped several bills down on the table. I barely counted it though I'm sure he got a hefty tip out of it. I took my girl's hand and walked her to my car for a night of quiet, slow sex and a million cuddles to remember forever.

Planes flew overhead and horns beeped in the background and my time with Ella dwindled down to moments. Her eyes shone with reserved tears and her lips quivered hearing my words. She was everything to me. More than my career and more than my own heart. I had to tell her what my heart begged for.

"Ella, if you think for one iota that you would like to further our relationship, please, go home and think about what that would look like. I already have and I know that I couldn't imagine it unless you were with me. You are my heart. My light. My love. I wanted you from the moment you asked if I was okay. You are a giver, the kindest person I've ever met. You…remind me of Irina and her big heart. I love you, El.

Please, consider a life with me and if you do, I'll be the happiest man in the world."

I slid my hands into her hair and brought her lips to mine tracing every inch of them and feeling the warmth of her breath on my skin. Our lips locked and our kiss filled everything my words couldn't produce. Her hands wound around my neck and I reached down to pull her up to my full height pressing every part of my being into her luscious form.

I heard a throat clearing behind me and I reluctantly pulled back my lips. She hummed licking her lips. "You sure know how to say goodbye to a girl." Her blush spread down to her chest.

"I know that's a pretty big ask but you should know, I don't think I can picture anyone else in my life. You do things to me I can't explain." My eyes began to well. "I wish we had more time. This wasn't long enough."

She looked at my driver who annoyingly pointed to his watch. "I will go home, but I won't like it. I need you, Viktor. Now and forever." She threw her arms around my neck pulling me tightly to her chest. "I'll always be there for you, Viktor. Please give your parents my best. I–love you." Her voice caught in her throat and my resolve not to cry broke and I damn nearly crushed her.

"I love you too, baby."

Our time was up and I passed her rolling luggage over to her with a swat on her behind.

"Text me when you land, and when you get back to your apartment." I gave her an electric smile that I hoped would be enough until we met again.

I was agitated, annoyed, and anxious. All the "A" words. Not even fifteen minutes after Ella left, I got a call from my agent telling me to get to his office immediately. I knew it wasn't good since it was Sunday and Leonard Schwartz would rather eat glass than work on a Sunday.

"What's going on," I demanded as we met in the lobby and rode the elegant elevator to his office.

He tossed back his head to finish his coffee and rounded his desk taking a seat before responding to me.

"I just got a call from a journalist friend who was leaving LAX and noticed you groping a brown-haired woman." His eyebrows arched and his smile wanted to know if I finally found "a hot piece of ass," his words, not mine.

"Calm yourself, Leonard. That woman will be my wife one day if I have my way." I raised my eyebrows right back at him. I slid more comfortably into my chair knowing that something terrible wasn't happening.

He choked trying to swallow. "Wife?" Leonard ejected himself from his seat and almost slid over the top of his desk to perch himself in front of my chair. "When did this happen? Where is she from? How did this slip by me?"

I laughed as I watched him throw a fit. "Calm down. I met her online. I've vetted her and even hired a private investigator to check her out to make sure she wasn't a lunatic fan. She's really amazing, Leonard. I can't live without her."

He scrubbed his face supposedly trying to understand the bomb I dropped on him. Typically, it was Leonard shoving a hot model or young actress onto my arm for whatever Hollywood bullshit event he felt would help my image. It's true that some of these women offered me more than a few photos for a tabloid spread. It's also true that with the exception of one woman, I only gave a friendly, if not perfunctory, kiss on the cheek to make the fans happy. I learned early on how vapid some of these people, women, and men, could be and I wasn't going to get my ass in a sling along the way. I loved what I did, but not enough to damage my name or that of my family.

Leonard walked towards the windows that faced the Los Angeles River. If I've learned anything from him it was while he was thinking I needed to shut up. Five minutes of checking out fingernails and realizing it was time for a manicure, that I need to stretch out more, and that as soon as I got out of this meeting, I'd have dozens of roses sent to Ella on Monday afternoon at work. I wanted everyone to know that she was mine and was loved so intensely that they should be jealous of her.

I heard a loud clap and that was my signal to start paying attention.

"Okay. So, here's the plan. I want her interviewed and we can put our own spin on how you met, why she was in L.A. and your intentions for your relationship. Yeah?" His freakish joker-like smile and nodded as his head awaited my reply.

"Uh, no." I pressed my lips together.

"No? Why not? What's wrong with that plan?" He scowled dropping his hands to his hips and shifting back in forth nervously.

"Because I don't need to do damage control. I don't need her life turned upside down with a world of voyeurs or paparazzi barricading her front door. She's an innocent bystander to my life and I won't have her paraded around to make other people happy." Now *I* was up pacing around the room.

"Listen, Viktor. I get it. You're in love and you're trying to protect your woman and her privacy. This is showbusiness. Your fans expect a story and your image of a single bachelor is being blown up. Your hotness level just skyrocketed. You are on the cusp of millions of women, and men, doing whacky things for one last ditch effort to pull you out of marriage. They want to be the one to have you. You're pulling the rug out from under them and if you don't give them something to sink their teeth into, all hell is going to break loose."

I froze in my path. The way Ella and I met broke my trust with my talent agent, my PR agent, my assistant, and perhaps one of my contracts. I'm not sure. I was culpable in this story and inadvertently put Ella in the limelight without her consent. *Christ!* I need to speak with her as soon as she lands. I grabbed my phone and sent her a text to call me when she saw this. My head dropped back and I closed my eyes in irritation. I needed to fix this without damaging our new and fragile relationship.

"There are a few things I should share with you before you decide what our next steps are. You aren't going to like what I'm about to tell you though so you'll have to get over it." I gestured to Leonard to take his seat and walked with my head hanging low back to mine. I proceeded to tell him the whole story without the intimate details. After each new twist in the story, you could see him wilting farther and farther in his seat. Truth be told, I did too. "So, now you see, we can't exactly broadcast my text conversations and the rest of it. I'm sure we can make up something more realistic or heartfelt, right? How about we met when we were kids and she moved to Wisconsin with her family and we ran into each other on a Zoom thing? Surprisingly good, huh?" I pushed forward onto my seat pressing my hands together in between my knees praying he'd buy it and therefore the public would as well.

"Damn, that's good. So wholesome and unexpected. I'll need to research her youth–schools, activities, etc., but this just might work. I'm sure your immigration situation will emerge soon so it wouldn't be unlikely that she would come into town to support you and you would show her around town. Viktor, why didn't you say something to me earlier? We could have managed the optics so much better."

He was right. I should have stayed between the rails like I was instructed, but then I never would have met Ella. Something within me said, "Take a chance. Live a little," and I did, and man was I living my best life now. It was astonishing how she listened to me and nurtured me this past weekend like Irina used to do. She had my back and said all the right things to calm me down and give me hope. I wondered if Irina sent her to me. Was she waiting to intervene in my life again? This couldn't have simply been serendipity, it seemed like a higher power was at work. Whatever the reason, I wasn't taking it for granted. I needed her on a cellular level and would do whatever was necessary to keep her.

I took a deep breath and laid everything on the line with Leonard. He'd either work with me or without me, either way, I was planning a future with Ella in it and nothing would get in my way to make that happen.

"Leonard. You know I've listened to your advice all these years, and I've played the mysterious heartthrob to build myself a top-notch brand as you requested. You've provided me opportunities I couldn't even imagine and I'm so grateful for your perseverance and guidance as I navigated the Hollywood scene."

"But..." he interjected.

"But nothing! I love acting. I love the creative space it provides and the talent I get to work with is astounding. I am truly blessed. I want Ella to be at my side for all of it though if she has to expose every iota of her life to the public, I don't want to do this anymore. She is that important to me." I didn't realize how much she permeated my being until now. Would I give up everything for her? Would she want me to? *Shit! I am so screwed.*

He got up from his seat and sat down in the chair beside me. His fatherly posture along with his graying cropped hair made me feel secure. He always knew when to get down to eye level and deliver his best lines. I was ready for them—I think.

"Let's put a pin in this until we, and I mean we, speak with Ella this evening. It's only fair she hears what is coming her way and we'll need a minute to process it all. If we're lucky she'll be along for the ride, let's wait and see. In the meantime, go write your backstory so she can read and edit it. I'll spend the rest of my *Sunday* researching your lady."

We both stood and uncharacteristically Leonard leaned in for a man-hug. Stunned, I stood there a moment before reciprocating.

"I'm so fucking happy for you, Vik. You deserve the absolute best. I'm proud of you."

Damn. That felt good.

CHAPTER 14

ELLA

My plane landed late Sunday evening and the same driver Viktor hired to take me was standing at the exit waiting to bring me home. I'd never been treated so well in my life. I could get used to this. I was at my door when I realized I needed to take my phone off airplane mode. It sounded like an arcade with all the bells and whistles going off like a machine gun once it was operational. It was embarrassing.

This guy didn't need to hear my conversations so I decided to wait until I got into my apartment before I answered any of them. My mind was whirring about everything that transpired this past weekend. First, Viktor's immigration meeting, then meeting his parents, then finding out about his dead sister. So much to digest. Oh, and let's not forget the introduction-to-porn sex. That was a revelation. I knew before going to L.A. that his hotness didn't end with his piercing eyes and stunning good looks. I had noticed his not-so-suggestive comments all along and knew he was an alpha wrapped in sheep's clothing. But when he strutted across the room full of swagger buck naked, my pussy gushed for his attention. And when he looked like he could eat me for dinner, my legs felt bandy and jellified. All that was awe-inspiring, though, when his raspy, sexy, Ukrainian accent emerged, I became electrified. I took pride in making his impressive cock mold into his jeans and I often wondered how uncomfortable it made him since he always was aroused when we were together.

 I entered my apartment and turned on some lights, dropped my bag next to my bedroom door, and went to the kitchen to get some water and figure out what to make for dinner. I filled the coffee pot full of water for tomorrow's breakfast and prepared the only thing in my refrigerator, bread and jelly. I dropped two slices of multi-grain into the toaster and grabbed the chunky peanut butter before I shot off three texts letting my mom, sister, and Rose know that I was back and would talk with them later. I confirmed a couple of appointments for my haircut and my oil change this week, when I saw the text from Viktor to call him immediately when I landed, my stomach dropped.

 I cued up his number and waited for him to answer. One ring was all it took.

 "Hey, baby. Thanks for calling back. How was your flight?" I could tell he was wound up. He knew I didn't call for small talk.

"Hey, yourself. The flight was good. What's wrong? Are your parents all right?" I just saw him six hours ago. What the hell happened since I left?

"No, sweetheart, they're fine, but I think I made a big mistake." Red flags were waving and gongs were going off in my head, and suddenly I felt nauseated. Please tell me he didn't think *we* were a mistake.

"Mistake? What do you mean? Did I do something wrong?" He must have reconsidered or his agent told him to dump me. Or his parents didn't think I was good enough for him.

"No, no, no. Let me start again. I should have said that my weekend with you was perfect–you're perfect. Perfect for me in every way. El, I made the mistake of not being completely honest with you about our relationship mostly because it won't only be us. My fans, this business, have their noses in everything I do, and being with me will mean that not only the fans will want to know who you are but so will the press. Details that they have no right to know but will pry until they get some answers. I should have explained how invasive dating an actor can be and although today isn't an issue, tomorrow could be." His voice sounded dejected and my heart broke for us both.

I was at a loss for what to say. The ugly truth was that he was right. I was so wrapped up in discovering each other that I wasn't thinking about who he was or what he did. We were having fun. We were in love.

"Baby, listen. We can work this out. There has to be a way. You do, want, to make this work, right?" My voice stuttered getting the words out. I didn't want this to end.

His deep sigh had me concerned. "Ella, my love. There is nothing more important to me than being with you, we have to work out a plan to protect each other. Since you left, I've been with my agent hashing out options, and I believe we have a solution though we'll have to do some digging into your past to be sure our facts line up. Would you be okay with that?" The pregnant pause as I processed his words triggered a fight or flight response and I knew that a decision had to be made now.

"El. Are you still there." He said urgently.

"Yes–find the facts you need to make this story stick. I only ask if you need to fabricate anything let me know first. I'll have to incorporate those into my vernacular."

"Thank God. Thank you! Give me a second to send Leonard, my agent, your permission."

I chugged my water and stood up. I was too amped to sit any longer.

"Okay. I've written out our story of how we met and why you were in town. Can I read it to you?"

"Sure," I said, getting back up to make my sandwich, I was too fidgety to sit after all. When he finished, I was surprised at how naturally he had us meeting and coming back together. I wouldn't have to change much of anything in our story and it was impressively believable. The only people who knew it wasn't the truth were his parents, my sister, and my parents, and none of them would ever implicate us.

"Well done, Viktor. You should write for a living." My nerves were jittery and I didn't know what to say next.

"I'm sorry to say, this is only the beginning. I want you to take a few days and really think about whether dating someone in the limelight is going to be a way of life you can tolerate. Think about all the other celebrities you've seen in People Magazine or any other Hollywood rag. The paparazzi might hound you or your family. They are relentless and sometimes terrifying. I can't make this decision for you though I can offer a bodyguard if you feel you need it. I loved our bubble and wish we could stay there but reality bites." I could see him in my head, rubbing his face and turning inward in his despair. Why did this need to be so hard?

"Wow. I never thought about any of this. You have always been my main focus in our relationship. I wasn't even thinking about all the other stuff you said. I know that sounds naïve but I always felt safe with you, even when I wasn't one hundred percent sure it was you until you sent me a picture of you in bed. By the way, I still look at it every day." I smiled into the phone and hoped that he heard my optimism.

"My dirty girl. God how I want to wrap you in my arms right now. I miss you so much." His voice accented all the good parts.

I whispered, "Viktor, we have to find a way to make this work. We must."

"Think about what I said and I'll get back to you as quickly as possible with our story details. My agent has always had my back and is happy that I found such a wonderful woman to love." I heard kissing sounds and a feint, "I love you so much," in the distance.

"I will. I'm here for you, Viktor, always. I love you too." I whispered back and he hung up.

VIKTOR

This woman! That's all I could think about. She didn't go running for the hills like I thought she might. She barely flinched at the unimaginable intrusions waiting to enter her life. She only thought of me. Unselfishly. Constant. Compassionate. How would I make this work?

It was time to vet out her past and stitch together a believable story. It was time to decide how far I would let my lifestyle interfere with her relatively simple life back in Wisconsin. And, most importantly, how did I get her to move here permanently? I needed her in my bed with me deep inside her every night. She loved me experimenting with various positions, timings, and toys. She loved it all and begged for more. A guy couldn't get any luckier than that. I picked up my phone and dialed Leonard to see where we stood.

"We're doing this Leo. Build the story, vet her past, and make us look like two stupid puppies who can't live without each other. Oh, and be sure to note that our parents were acquainted early on. I want everyone who knows to be involved so that there aren't any loose ends."

I was so ecstatic waiting for his reply that I almost knocked over my beer.

"Good job, Vik. Now, how and when do we get her here permanently?" He was pressuring me again and knew it was his job to do so.

"I should have an answer about her commitment to dealing with all this Hollywood crap in a day or two. I don't want to pressure her like you're pressuring me. Got it? In the meantime, I'm heading over to my parents to share with them my story in case anyone bangs on their door."

We hung up and I put in a call to my folks to let them know I was on my way. We debriefed the whole situation including the information she learned about Irina. By the time I left, we had covered all eventualities and they wanted to make Ella feel as much like family as soon as possible. I gave them her number and left for the gym. I was wound so tight I almost cracked my back teeth.

I sat in my bed later that evening and prayed for a miracle when my phone pinged on the app Ella and I met on.

El30MG: Is this Viktor Zolof?

My girl was being cute. Okay. I'll play along.

ME: Yeah, this is Viktor. Who is this?

An image opened it immediately. The picture only showed her bowed mouth glossed over in cherry red with her pointy finger laid over her bottom lip.

El30MG: Shh! Don't tell anyone that you found my pussy in your bed this past weekend. The paparazzi can never know.

Fuck!

ME: I promise not to say anything if you keep bringing me that sweet mound back to me.

Another image appeared and my jaw dropped.

El30MG: This sweet pussy?

She wore a barely-there soft pink piece of lace over her bared mound with her finger slipped over her clit. *Damn, what a tease.*

ME: Yeah, baby, that one. I can taste you on my tongue right now.

Another ping, but with a video request. A nanosecond later I clicked on it holding my breath for what I might see.

El30MG: Take a closer look.

Her pussy was glistening with her essence as she pulled her panties down.

ME: Spread your legs wider and let me see all of you.

El30MG: I want you Viktor. Now and always. My answer is yes and you'll come with me tonight to seal our future. Do you understand, big boy?

ME: Completely.

I yanked the covers back, set the phone down while I tore my boxer briefs off, and grabbed my pulsing cock as I picked the phone back up.

"Damn El. You are so beautiful. I want you to come so hard for me."

"I never want another cock but yours. You are absolutely filthy and I love it!" she growled.

"That mouth! God, I love that mouth. I'm fantasizing about it being on my dick as we speak." I moaned as I pulled harder on my leaking shaft.

"Oh, my God! Yes, Vik. I love how you taste. I love how you always know what to do and how to do it. I love you, baby!" The arch in her back held testament to her increasing pleasure. Her moans were exquisite and I couldn't hold back any longer.

"I love you too. I'm coming, baby. Come with me now." I begged.

I spurted into my hand so hard imagining her mouth sucking every drop. The images of her face etched into my brain from this weekend were so vivid that I'd never forget her big, hooded eyes staring at me with adoration. *Fuck what I wouldn't do to have her with me now.*

"Baby, that was so intense. So. Fucking. Hot. I don't know if I can wait to see you again."

"I was thinking the same exact thing." She smiled and licked the finger she used to come. *Tease!*

We sat there unmoving, staring at each other piecing together the next part of our lives like a movie we both starred in. I needed to ask another difficult question though the timing would be rushed. I had to take the chance and hoped for the best, nonetheless.

"My beautiful, Ella. Would you consider moving to L.A. and becoming my permanent girlfriend? I don't want to freak you out and I know it's a big ask, but…"

"And by permanent girlfriend, do you mean wife?" Her eyes were big and her breath was held tightly in her chest.

"Well, when you put it like that…" I got down on one knee, naked and afraid, and said those magical words that changed lives forever, "Ella Genereau, the love of my life, will you marry me?"

The corners of her mouth quirked and then the corners spread to her eyes, "Viktor, my love. It is a big ask. You hardly know me. I could bite my toenails with my mouth or blow my nose into the sink instead of a tissue. Are you sure you want to take that chance?"

She was stifling a laugh and so was I. She knew me well enough that I would praise her bendiness being able to bite her toenails with her mouth, and, well, we could work on the nose-blowing thing. Most importantly, she wanted me to take a beat and truly understand what I was asking for, and when our eyes locked on each other again, I nodded.

"Yes, beautiful lady. I'll take a chance on your nose and your toes and everything in between. Especially all the stuff in-between." I raised the screen to my lips and kissed her back.

"Yeah, you have some ridiculous stuff in-between as well." She bit her lip and flipped over onto her tummy. "You should know that my job is transferable, so I can keep working in my field when I get to L.A. Nurses are in need everywhere. I'll need to give my notice here and tie up some loose ends but I could potentially be there in a month or so. I wonder where I'd live. With your parents or somewhere else?"

"Ha! You're hilarious. My bed. That's where you'll live for weeks before I let you out of my sight." He threw his head back and laughed deeply, making my chest hum. I loved her sense of humor and levity during difficult times. I'll need that. We have a lot to work out and so long as she trusted me, I knew we could navigate through anything." Her smile was contagious and I beamed my approval back at her.

I jumped up off the floor and danced around the room. I must have put on quite a show since I heard her yell, "Tuck that shit in!"

"Oh, sweetheart. You've made me so happy. I promise to make this as painless as possible. I'll cover all the costs and have movers pack all your shit up. Whatever you need, just say the word." I collapsed back onto the end of my bed. "I can't believe you said yes," I muttered to myself.

She brought her screen close to her mouth and kissed it. "You better believe it."

Two socially awkward goofballs who found satisfaction online—a million to one shot. They will believe one thing though; we were meant to be with one another. Our love was made in the heavens waiting for the right moment to shine."

EPILOGUE

ELLA

My parents were flabbergasted. Rosie, my Charge Nurse, was, "Atta girl," and my roommate said she wanted to redecorate. Tell me, why was I making this move such a big deal? I loved my parents except getting them to understand how modern dating worked was more akin to explaining how combustion worked on a rocket ship. The only person who truly was angry was my sister.

"I don't understand why you can't take me with you. I promise I won't drool on your man. I'm reformed." Her begging was endearing especially when she referred to my last boyfriend and his drool-worthy smile. *I did miss that panty-looking quirk he made with his pillowy lips.*

"It's still a hard no for me, sis. Maybe you can talk to your perfect husband to move you out to L.A. and we can put a bib back on you. Viktor promised he'd fly me home twice a year so you wouldn't forget about me." I shoved the last of my shoes into a box and tape-gunned it closed. The movers were coming any minute and I promised them I'd be ready.

"You better remember that I get to be your matron of honor when you get married." She put her hands on her hips and gave me her don't-mess-with-me stare.

I walked into the kitchen, sister in tow. She was taking all my open food home and the rest to a local food bank. Sadly, there wasn't much in my pantry to give. I did, however, have one last bottle of wine that we never had time to split, waving it in front of her eyes.

"Yeah, yeah. You've got the job. Besides, I won't have friends worthy of that job. My current work friends will forget about me in three months, and they'll only remember me because they have more shifts to cover." I unscrewed the cap, *I'm classy that way*, took a long swig, and passed the bottle to my sister. She wiped the top with her arm, like that was going to help keep the germs from infiltrating her mouth and glugged a few times herself.

My phone rang and my gorgeous fiancé's face appeared.

"Hey, baby girl, ready for your flight?" He purred.

"Uh, that's my cue to leave," Missy hugged me tightly and kissed my forehead. "I love you so much. Call me for anything and everything." I hugged her back and pushed her hair behind her ears.

"You know I will. I love you, Missy. Give my niece and nephew a big smooch, and, maybe one for Dennis." We had one more sister-to-sister moment and she grabbed the grocery bags and left yelling over her shoulder.

"Goodbye, Viktor. You'd better take care of my sister or I'll kill you–right after I jump your bones." She laughed all the way down the hall.

"I haven't even met her yet, and I love her. Of course, I love you the most." He assured me.

"You better!" I laughed back. I walked around the rest of the apartment checking to be sure everything of mine had been collected. I left my beloved couch and queen-sized bed for my roommate only as my parting gift to her. I didn't need anything besides Viktor to start my new life and I was all too ready for it to begin.

"I have several surprises for you when you arrive so don't miss your plane. The movers texted me they are on their way and my driver will be there at eight to get you on your red eye. I miss you so fucking bad, El." He went from sounding like a child about the surprise, to professional about the logistics. I knew this move was a rollercoaster, it's just that I didn't stop to consider how much all these changes would affect him. We needed time to acclimate to each other. Time to feel each other out without the pressure of work and family. I hope one of my surprises was a quarantine at his apartment for a week so we could do all the bedroom things we've been missing.

"Viktor."

"Yes, sweetheart."

"Is this still what you want? If it isn't just say so. We can slow this all down. I don't want you to think I'm pressuring you in any way." I paced around the coffee table rubbing my forehead when I heard a knock at the door. "This is your last chance to back out. The moving guys are standing behind my apartment door."

One breath. Two breaths. Three breaths. Four breaths.

"With all my heart. With all my soul. I want you, Ella Genereau. So much." I heard the hiccup in his voice. The love and the pain of not being together for the past month were taking their toll. He did love me, I knew this. Unconditionally.

"I want you too." The knock then turned into a series of bangs.

"Coming!" I yelled. "I love you, Viktor. I'll text you when I'm on the plane."

VIKTOR

I called my decorator as soon as Ella's plans to move were in place. I had two weeks to transform my apartment into something my beautiful lady would feel was hers, too.

"I want color, Emily. Not overly bright, you know, soft and feminine. The bedroom needed a vanity table for her to put on her make-up. Please do something with my closet so she has room in there for all her things. Come to think of it, we may need to expand that later. Oh, and a pretty dresser for her things. Basically, work your magic and send me the bill." I smiled and walked her to the door.

"Besides the hardware, it's on me. You made my career, Viktor. It's the least I could do." She kissed me on both cheeks and cat-walked out of my apartment like a trained femme fatal. Like a perfectly choreographed ballet, my phone pinged me with an email I'd been waiting for from UCLA.

Like a Pavlovian Dog, I went into the kitchen to grab a beer and sat at the island to read their message. *Yes!* Even though it's been six years since I was a student there, they would honor my credits. There were two classes that needed to be taken over since more relevant information is in the curriculum. That would mean I only had twenty credits to get my degree. *Why the hell did I wait so long to do this?* I emailed the Registrar and set an appointment to meet with them in person along with the Dean of the Public Health department. I didn't want my attending classes to distract their other students and hoped many of those credits could be taken online. Ella would be ecstatic about this opportunity for us both and I couldn't wait to share this news with her. It would give us options when or if I needed to end my acting career. I would do anything for her–anything.

It was time to get my girl, and like before, I had arrived coffee in hand along with another special surprise. After parking the car, I entered the baggage area looking for my girl only to see her with one foot on the conveyor frame and two hands on a handle, I could see the strain on her face as she tried to wrangle the giant suitcase and couldn't help but rush to her aide. So adorable.

"Excuse me, Ma'am. Can I help you with those?" I drawled for effect.

She didn't even lift her head when she spoke, "Yes, please. If my stupid boyfriend was here like he said would I wouldn't have had to deal with this myself."

I gave her a second to feel my hand on her lower back before she lifted her head to see who touched her inappropriately. "Stupid, huh? Should I step aside and let some other handsome available actors help you instead?" I couldn't suppress my smile. I'd never seen her so riled up.

She blew a fallen lock of hair from her messy bun and shot back, "Fine. You'll do." And flung herself around my neck. I wish I could have hugged her back but my hands were still pulling her luggage to the ground. I kissed her between pulling off the next two pieces and then wheeled us off to the car.

"You need to be fed and watered, Missy." I loved keeping a scene alive.

And like the hidden actress she'd become, she replied, "I do, and don't call me Missy." I threw my head back at her comedic timing. "That's my sister, and she isn't invited to this little reunion." My face hurt with all the smiling we did as we drove to our favorite breakfast spot. Being silly with Ella was like being on a carousel; the music kept playing even through the ups and downs.

An hour later we arrived at my apartment, correction—our apartment, and Ella flipped out with all the décor changes. Marianna was cleaning up the kitchen from preparing us lunch and dinner and stopped what she was doing to hug and welcome Ella back for good. I gave her the rest of the day off because let's face it, me and my girl were getting horizontal and staying that way for a long time.

I walked her around the apartment pointing out where her things would go when I pressed her to her new mercury glass-covered dresser.

"Let's play a game. You open each drawer and then take off a piece of clothing, starting with this one." I pointed to the drawer at the top right.

"Ooh. I love games. She reached inside and pulled out a small box from Cartier. I hoped she wasn't disappointed when she opened it but when she saw the one-karat diamond studs gleaming back at her I knew she loved them.

"Oh my god, Vik! They're huge! You shouldn't have." Her hands cupped the box and she jumped into my arms. I grabbed her ass and pulled her tighter into me. If I had my way, she would never leave them.

"They certainly aren't as beautiful as you are, El, and definitely not as valuable to me either. Now take off your shirt and open that drawer." I indicated the top left drawer was next.

She dropped her feet and slowly pulled off her V-neck t-shirt letting it drop to the floor. She winked at me then reached with her right hand to pull the drawer open and pulled out an envelope. Her eyes scrunched up. "It's from UCLA. What's this?"

"Open it." I rubbed circles all along her back getting soft moans from her frequently. I nuzzled into kissing her neck as she reached both hands around my head to read it.

I heard the envelope flip open and drop to the floor as the paper unfolded in her hands.

It is with great pleasure that you are accepted back into the Public Health Undergraduate Program at UCLA this fall. As per our conversation with Dean Perth, you will be required to re-take two clinical disease courses bringing your eventual diploma current with known medical knowledge and fifteen additional credits to complete your program. Congratulations, and welcome back to being a Bruin.

"Are you serious?! You're going back to school? Why?" She sounded hysterical though I couldn't tell if it was motivated by happiness or peril.

"Very serious, El. I've always wanted to finish my degree. Remember, my getting into acting was a fluke. I want us to have options in case this lifestyle becomes too much for both of us. Being with you is the only thing I want. An actor's life is fickle. One day you're hot, the next you're not. Haters. Intruders. All that shit. I want to be prepared, for us and our future family." I slid my hands into her soft chestnut waves and gently pulled her head back. I watched her face turn pink and her eyes well with unshed tears. I kissed her deeply, impressing upon her my devotion to her while tasting her salty tears. When I pulled away, I changed the tone immediately.

"Take off your pants. Then kneel down." *Shit! That even made me wet.* She did, and I pointed to the lower left drawer. "Open it."

She licked her lips and gave me the sexiest look I'd ever seen.

"So bossy." She reached over to find a drawer full of sex toys and the gasp out of her mouth was one of my presents for the day. "All of those? For me?" She laughed knowing I knew how much she enjoyed being pushed out of her comfort zone.

"Yes, baby, and for me. I plan on making you come a hundred ways from Sunday." She didn't wait for the next drawer. Instead, she unbuttoned my jeans and yanked both my pants and underwear down releasing my hard weeping cock.

"I can't wait, Viktor. Just a taste, please." She looked up at me, not for permission but to see my eyes glaze over like they did every time she took me into her wet mouth.

"Such a dirty girl. Do it. Suck me." She didn't disappoint me. Our game was paused while she greedily took me to the back of her throat. The sounds she made were too much for me. It had been far too long for me to keep myself together. "You are so fucking good at that." I tried to steady my breath. I tried to think straight. This woman was a treasure I'd never lose.

"Baby, stop. I won't last and I want you to open your last drawer. I watched her roll over to the right pushing her ass in the air as she went. If she thought tempting me with her curvy cheeks, she would be okay, she didn't plan on my smack to her ass leaving a pink stain for me to enjoy.

"Hey!" She sounded so indignant.

"Hey, yourself. You don't need to tempt me, beautiful. I already want you. Now open the damn drawer and look inside." I stepped back and gave her some space to do my bidding.

She looked confused. "Another envelope?" This one was unmarked and she tore it open, not making a sound. Her eyebrows drew together and her lips mouthed each word she read intently.

She jumped up shaking the paper in the air. "Is this for real? It's over? You and your family are free to keep your citizenship? It's dated weeks ago." Her eyes were wide and her mouth was still red from her ministrations.

I felt sheepish keeping this from her for two weeks but seeing her expression was worth it. My immigration papers were fixed, filed, and forgotten by the U.S. Government. I could leave the state or the country. My parents were so relieved that they planted ten American flags all around their house.

"Yes, to all of it. I'm back to being a legal citizen. Thank God that's over." I pulled her into my arms squeezing her tightly. "Thank you for standing by my side through all of it. I'll never forget it." We kissed slowly for several minutes before I pulled her away from me.

"There is one more gift I have for you, if you want it, that is." I waggled my eyebrows and walked her over to my nightstand. With her tits on display, and my dick getting hard again, I reached into the drawer and pulled out a red velvet box. She gasped.

"Viktor, you already bought me jewelry." Time stood still and I looked into her red blotchy face, my beautiful girl's face. She was perfect no matter what hue she was.

"Ella. My love. You lifted my soul when I was lost and lonely. You brightened my life every day that I've known you. You've shown me loyalty and understanding when others only wanted to take that from me. I want to spend the rest of my life showing you how much I love you, admire you, and respect you. I want to share everything with you, beautiful lady. You have been the most important swipe of my life. Would you please be my wife?"

One breath. That's all it took.

"YES! A million times, yes."

THE END

Acknowledgments

This story is just one that so many of us wish could happen to us. Taking a risk and having it pay off in a way we could never dream of. Although risky, I did my own social "stalking" and found that even when you think you're speaking with a live person, you probably aren't speaking with the person you hoped to converse with. It was fun though. Exciting and full of fantastical opportunities. Good thing I knew it was all a farce and just had fun with the process. BE CAREFUL OUT THERE!

The people that make all these crazy ideas come to life are YOU, and all your encouragement. I love writing these stories to give you hope, encouragement, a kick in the pants, or whatever you need to love life as it comes to you.

To My Peeps:

Daryl – I look forward to when you finish each of my novels. Enough said. Thank you for taking time out of your remarkably busy schedule to give me your best feedback. I love you.

Sam – Thanks for your hugs while I'm deep into my writing groove, and for letting me test out my sometimes-raunchy dialogue.

Evan—What would the world do without you? Probably never see my website, or have a form to fill out, or bring me joy every time we Google Meet. I love you.

Jennifer Haskin – Always ready to step in and hold my hand, bend her ear, or just share life as it happens. I'm so happy to have you in mine.

Megan Zinn – For always keeping me out of the weeds.

Fran – Thanks for taking the time to promote me to everyone you know and sending praises when they are needed most.

And, to all my friends who have to keep hearing about my writing process…you complete me.

THANK YOU, MY INSATIABLE READERS!

About the Author:

The sassy and sensational Beth Gelman is a professional pianist and vocalist and has authored her third steamy romance. Authentic, resilient, loyal, and spiritual, she's not afraid to learn, fail, speak her mind, or try new things. She loves writing romances, especially romances that make her readers grow and appreciate their strengths and weaknesses. She loves her lattes, yoga, and every dog on the planet, and especially her devoted husband. This is her fourth book. You can find out more about her here: www.BethGelman.com.

YOUR OPINION MATTERS TO ME!

I would love to hear what you thought about Socially Satisfied at

www.Amazon.com/dp/B0BWFWBVKN

GoodReads.com, or Bookbub.com.

You can also follow me on:

Facebook: Beth Gelman's Insatiable Readers

Instagram: @BethGelmanWrites

TikTok/BookTok: authorbethgelman

Sign-up for my Newsletter at:

BethGelmanWrites@gmail.com

for fun, freebies and more!

What's Next?

Now it's time to catch up on <u>The Perfect Series</u>!

Have you read **The Perfect Voice** and **The Perfect Lessons**? Here's a chapter to get you started.

The final book in the series, **Making Perfect Sense**, arrives on Amazon.com in **August 2023**. PRE-ORDER your copy today.

<u>www.Amazon.com/dp/B0BRWP5857</u>

Sneak Peek: The Perfect Voice

The Perfect Voice

BETH GELMAN

Chapter 1

RUBY

"Oh My God, Trudie, I just can't do it anymore! I'm so tired of asshole bosses disrespecting and taking advantage of me."

My poor friend sat by while I mourned yet another epic work failure. Trudie passed me a third glass of wine. "Come on," she said, "don't give up yet."

I was trying to figure out where my life went sideways. I couldn't believe I was back living in my parents' suburbia home in the Midwest after another dismal attempt at "adulting." This most recent marketing position was a step outside my comfort zone, but once again, I was let go for some contrived reason.

I racked my brain trying to find a thread that connected the last two positions I'd held and lost. All I knew was my ideas and contributions were recognized and praised by my immediate supervisors and that both misogynistic bosses thanked me for my ideas, took credit for the projects' success, and then "unfortunately" let me go.

As per usual, security marched me over to human resources to sign some papers and hear a "good-bye/good luck" scripted speech. "We don't want to get into the 'weeds,'" the HR rep stuttered out. Weeds? What the hell was that? Did that mean my boss was threatened by me? That's crap!

Disgusted with corporate bullshit and my lack of control in the world, I stormed out of the HR office carrying my one box of pictures, a "*No Hablo El Stupido*" coffee mug, my Groot bobblehead, and the sock monkey plush that Trudie gave me when I landed the job.

Nearing the front reception desk, I heard mumblings of why I was let go from Dumb and Dumber, the two bimbos that sat there every day, filing their nails and batting their eyes at every Y chromosome they encountered, instead of doing their fucking jobs.

"I heard she slept with her boss," Dumb said to Dumber.

"OMG! I overheard she was leaking company secrets to our competitors," Dumber said to Dumb.

Whipping around to face the reception counter, I screamed "FUCK YOU! I've heard you're both raving bitches, but I'm not talking behind your backs!" at the two receptionists who loved to see one of their own fail. "Or...maybe...again, my jackass boss stole my work and passed it off as his own! I'm through with this bullshit! Perhaps you two lackeys should stop sucking your bosses' dicks to get ahead."

I was out of control and these girls were in the line of my wrath. *Too fucking bad!* Two years down the tubes, AGAIN! Christ, why can't women have great ideas and get recognized for their contributions instead of their male bosses stealing their work? *UGH!*

∞

Placing my wineglass on my whitewashed nightstand covered with want ads and candy wrappers, I rolled onto my back in defeat. My fluffy white duvet with Madonna's *Vogue* album cover emblazoned on it flattened under my weight.

"Why does this keep happening to me?" I moaned as I hung my head off the side of my childhood bed.

I had been lucky as a kid. My mom fought hard with my dad to get me a full-sized bed when I turned thirteen. "My baby girl is growing up and needs a Big Girl Bed." Big girl, indeed! Now, look at me, crying like a baby, pity-drinking wine, and scarfing down Oreos, trying to pick up the crumbled cookies of my life (and the crumbs in my ample cleavage and bed sheets).

I had become a successful independent event planner even though I kind of fell into it after helping a friend out at her wedding. I had a different degree out of college, but not a vision of where I wanted to go and what I wanted to do with my life, so I pulled my resources together and became the Go to Girl Assistant, LLC. I was the master of my domain. From there, I spun off into work as an executive assistant. I helped one client for three years before I decided to work for another organization. My talents were praised and respected by my clients, and if I could have made enough money to move out of my parents' home, I would have kept that career. Hence, the recent decision to stay put in the safety of my parent's home, in beautiful Birmingham, Michigan, while I got settled into a long-term career.

Doing her best to offer support, Trudie, my best friend from college, had come over to shore me up. Lying alongside me, she propped herself up on her elbows with her cleavage pressed into Madonna's nose, closed her eyes, and sighed. She knew I needed to keep venting.

"Listen, Trudie. You know my parents are the best. They have always supported everything I've tried. They were the ones who shook the cowbell at my marching band shows, brought flowers to my recitals, and called the local newspaper to do an article about the beautiful weddings I did down on the Detroit River. But even my wonderful parents only have so much patience with me. I'm twenty-eight years old and if I have to hear, 'we know you're doing your best, Ruby, but…,' one more time, I'm going to scream!"

When my dad's eyes drooped after hearing that my best-laid plans had gone south, a piece of my heart died. My mom even started to leave magazine and newspaper clippings for job opportunities around. Subtle, and a little passive aggressive, I'd say, but I knew she did it out of love.

I had seen some pictures and notes she made about turning my bedroom into her dream crafting space while looking for some sheet music earlier that week. The soft blue curtains with tiny little cherries, white IKEA storage cubes, and a high-end sewing area were not going to happen until I moved out for good, which made my heart hurt. *Again, sorry to disappoint you, Mom.*

At breakfast that morning, my dad sat down at our worn maple kitchen table with his favorite hazelnut coffee in the "World's Best Dad" mug I had given him in third grade and a copy of the *Detroit Free Press*. As he took his first sip, he looked up at me and let out a breath. Yeah, I knew what was coming.

"Ya know, Ruby, your brother could use a little help at his accounting firm. Why don't you give him a call?" My dad turned slowly in his seat, and reaching for me, pulled me into his barrel chest, covered with his softest flannel shirt. I gazed over his broad shoulder and fought back the tears of yet another failure. To me, his words sounded like, "See how well your brother is doing? Why can't you be more like him?" Stepping away with leaky eyes and an attempt at a smile, I fled upstairs to my room. I wasn't sure how much lower my ego could go. Didn't Dad know that I was a creative person and Doug was more traditional and linear? I couldn't fit my square-peg self in a round hole any more than he could feel nuance. Why couldn't my parents see that?

Trudie sat up, arranged her legs crisscross style, and grabbed her wine off the nightstand. Do you know that look that a mama bear gives to a predator when her baby is in jeopardy? It has nothing on Trudie.

"All of those other careers have made you what you are today, Ruby," she soothed. "You loved being an event planner. You got to use all your creative juices, and it forced you to be organized. Your attention to detail is off the charts." She toasted into the air, spilling some wine on my comforter. Thank goodness it was a pinot grigio.

Trudie continued animatedly, "You were a President's Club saleswoman for two years, proving you are amazing at negotiating and persuading clients to buy whatever you were selling." She cocked her head to the side, giving me puppy dog eyes and then looked at the empty bottle. "Maybe we should switch to the hard stuff instead of opening another bottle of wine." She just wanted to get me wasted so I could forget my troubles. *Not a bad idea.*

I looked around my room and took in the awards and ribbons of my previously happy life. Trophies dusted with time, pictures of me and my bestie making glorious music, me on the piano at band concerts, and others singing at choir pop-concerts. I saw playbills from a high school performance of *The Music Man,* and thanks to my mom, my acceptance letter to attend a distinguished music school in Michigan. In retrospect, I should have known that my above-average abilities would only take me so far.

Maybe I had needed to take an extra "beat" when I chose to be a piano performance major? That probably would have been a better financial decision. But my high school senior recital and college auditions were amazing. I played an intricate Haydn Piano Sonata in F Major and a deeply moving Chopin Mazurka in A Minor, and I felt so accomplished and proud of the final product. I fantasized that I was destined to become another Horowitz or Cliburn.

These pieces were game changers for me. I hadn't played them in over two years, but whenever I heard the music, I was still deeply moved. Perhaps poetry in motion wasn't the best way to describe how I felt; maybe "the most erotic lovemaking you can think of" would fit the bill. *Which reminds me, I really need to get laid!*

"I'll never forget your audition, Ruby. You were so jubilant, confident, and proud of all the hard work you had put in. I can't remember you feeling that way about anything since then. What happened to that girl?" Trudie asked, as she licked her fingers to swipe the last Oreo crumbs out of the package.

Good question. Where did that girl go? I failed as a music major. I changed to business management but couldn't get through statistics and finance. What was I supposed to do after failing two majors by the time I was a senior, leaving me without a chance in hell of graduating in four years? Oh, and guess who was still paying for these "life lessons?" *Me!* I was drowning.

I sounded like a whiny bitch, but at the time, I was twenty-one years old and had no future to look forward to. I felt like a loser in my parents' eyes, although they'd never say that out loud, and I felt like a loser in mine because I kept changing my mind about a career. The only thing I had going for me was my resilience.

"Come on, Ruby! Pick yourself up, dust yourself off, and go find another degree to get the hell out of school," was my daily mantra.

So, I did what I should have done after my freshman year—I went to a guidance counselor. It was like seeing an accountant. You pushed all your receipts (or credits) in front of them and they would tell you what your net worth was. Well, good news! Not only did I have enough credits for a piano and voice minor, but I also had enough credits for a management minor too. *Yay me!* Except you can't graduate with three minors.

Suffice it to say, I found an area of study where I excelled and graduated with a Bachelor of Fine and Applied Arts with an emphasis in communications—on the five-year plan. Finally, I had a degree (and only $17,000 in debt). More importantly, I could move on to the next chapter of my life! Or home, as the case may be.

Crap! By the way, how does one monetize communications?

THAT'S ALL FOR NOW! Get your copy on Amazon.com today.

www.Amazon.com/dp/B09TS1YD5C

Read THE PERFECT LESSONS now for Trudie's Story

at: www.Amazon.com/dp/B0BSFX6JX7

and the end of the series in, MAKING PERFECT SENSE coming out August 2023

www.Amazon.com/dp/B0BRWP5857

Made in the USA
Columbia, SC
23 April 2024